HEXAGON:
THE WAR OF
THE IMMORTALS

Romain d'HUISSIER

HEXAGON:
THE WAR OF
THE IMMORTALS

Adapted by
Jean-Marc LOFFICIER

A Black Coat Press Book

ISBN 978-1-64932-102-2. First Publication: November 2021
Published by Black Coat Press c/o Hollywood Comics.com,
LLC, P.O. Box 17270, Encino, CA 91416, USA, under license
from Mosaic Multimedia. All characters of this book are © et
™ 2021 Mosaic Multimedia. All rights reserved. No similarity
between any of the names, characters, persons and/or institutions in this book with those of any living or dead person or
institutions is intended, and any such similarity which may
exist is purely coincidental. Except for review purposes, no
part of this book may be reproduced or transmitted in any
form or by any means, electronic or mechanical, including
photocopying, recording, or by any information storage and
retrieval system, without permission in writing from the pub-
lisher. Original novel © 2013 Romain d'Huissier/Mosaic Multimedia. English translation Copyright © 2021 Jean-Marc
Lofficier/Mosaic Multimedia. Cover illustration Copyright ©
2013 Amar Djouad/Mosaic Multimedia. The stories and characters depicted in this novel are entirely fictional. Printed in
the United States of America.

A Brief History of the Hexagon Group

Hexagon is a team of superheroes who came together to fight the threat of the alien tyrant Melanos of Zhud and his army of warlike reptilians, the Xans. The original group included Aster (also from Zhud) and his girlfriend Pinky, Jeff Sullivan (a.k.a. The Man of Brass), the Dark Flyer, the White Mask, the Mysterious Archer and Black Lys.[1]

After the White Mask left after the disastrous affair of the Dark Hive, he was replaced by astronaut Maximilian Worth, a.k.a. Max Tornado, who had accidentally gained superpowers on Mars. But Max soon became a reservist because of his duties at N.A.S.A. Mozam, from the African state of Benguela, then joined the group, adding his mystic skills to the group.

Dax, the original Mysterious Archer, was replaced by a second Mysterious Archer, Jukka Häyhä from Finland. After a fierce battle with Jeff's villainous brother, Fred "Blackie" Sullivan, Gun Gallon, who was exiled from his other-dimensional realm of Orios, joined the Group.[2]

Right after that, Hexagon faced Heptagon, a deadly cabal comprised of seven of their deadliest enemies. The French Guardian of the Republic arrived just in time to rescue them and was made an honorary member. He was soon joined by Miss Meteor from the negative universe of Zhud.

---

[1] See *Hexagon #1: The Dark Hive.*
[2] See *Hexagon #2: vs. Heptagon.*

Eventually, Cletus Nero, the first Dark Flyer, retired to be replaced by his son, Dominik. Gun Gallon returned to Orios and his seat was taken by Jeff Sullivan's daughter, Kathryn, a.k.a. Plasma. A new addition was Rakar, a former Marine and a descendent of the famous Lakota hero. Rakar first helped Hexagon against their archenemy, the Necromancer. Nevertheless, the villain managed to mind control the group, forcing them to battle the Strangers on the Moon. Jeff Sullivan died—or so we thought at the time.[3]

Following the death of its historic leader, the group went from failure to failure until they recruited "Blackie" Sullivan, who, seeking redemption, agreed to join and inherited the "Soul of Levan," the mystical power of their family that Jeff had held before him.

This new Hexagon, now comprised of Black Lys, Plasma, Rakar, the Mysterious Archer, the Dark Flyer and Blackie Sullivan then fought Ghool, the last Fomore, whose plans for world domination involved the destruction of the Earth's ecosystem. After a fierce battle, they triumphed and saved the world again.[4]

Expecting Rakar's child, Kathryn took maternity leave and was replaced by a young hero, Ben Leonard, a.k.a. Ra, whose strange past is at the center of the adventure that follows...

Now read on!

Jean-Marc Lofficier

---

[3] See *Strangers #1: Strangers in a Strange Land.*
[4] See *Hexagon: Dark Matter.*

PROLOGUE

The man was still. He was sitting on a metal throne, in the middle of a small, windowless room, with bare walls. He sat upright, his forearms resting on his thighs, his body slightly bent forward. His face was expressionless; his eyes gazed absent-mindedly at the door in front of him. He was barely breathing, his chest rising only very slightly.

His mind, too, was still. His thoughts seemed frozen, as if blocked by some unseen force. He still managed to think, but in slow motion—his brain was stuck. Every thought of his traveled along its synapses with great difficulty before reaching his neurons. It was painful; the ensuing migraine discouraged him from trying again. A barely audible sigh marked his defeat.

So the man turned to the past. He knew that the answer he sought rested somewhere in his memories. The answer to one crucial question, the only thought he had managed to formulate clearly: who was he and what was he doing here? But all the barriers imposed upon his brain made the exercise difficult. Still, this time, it mattered less. He had to know the truth.

He ransacked his failing memory. His handsome, well-drawn face became covered with a thin film of sweat as his will forced its way into his past. Fragments of memory exploded, crashing into his brain areas like shards of glass. A silent groan escaped from his lips. Pain and triumph combined.

He remembered! He had managed to assemble the jigsaw puzzle that were his memories, and file them in a roughly chronological order—at least, he thought so.

The effort had almost overwhelmed him. Despite his powerful frame, his body began to shake. Perspiration ran down his neck and onto his chest. His mind concentrated further and, eventually, blurred images started to acquire some sharpness.

The man had been a hero—of that, he was certain. Recurring scenes showed him fighting criminals and saving people. He had been admired. And he was not alone: he saw himself surrounded by other champions like him, the gods of a modern pantheon protecting the world against all threats. He visualized these: reptilian beings, an ageless man with ageless eyes, his own brother, darker than he was, more tormented. And still others: a long succession of evildoers whom he had fought in battles of cosmic dimensions!

But that's not all he was. He was also a husband and a father. He saw the face of his wife, then of his daughter; they were blurred, but he managed to invoke them. They shone with a golden glow; they were his guiding lights. A discreet tear ran down his cheek. He also saw a brother, another light, too: a good man like him, a hero in his own way. A shadow lurked behind this memory: another brother, perhaps? One who resembled him in a strange way, and who also shone, but with a dark glow—a black light.

The man sought to understand where he was, why he was in this state of confusion. His brow furrowed, his teeth gnashed. Suddenly, he saw another battle—his pantheon defeated, dominated. He saw himself captive, tortured. At the edge of his perception, he saw a desolate landscape: grey plains, tapering rocks, empty craters and an ink-black sky. Other gods stepped in that day, but he remained powerless against his executioner. He now recognized the Ageless Man, the Immortal. He had freed himself, somehow, and struck his would-be executioner. He had sacrificed himself in an explosion worthy of Ragnarok.

Then, he had died.

Suddenly, he stood up and looked around him. His memory told him he was in a world not very different from his own. He remembered that it has happened before: his spirit migrating through the dimensions to avoid its ultimate destruction. The plane of existence where he was now was at war. Once again, he saw hatred and death. He had risen to fight for peace and had managed to bring some order to this world in the midst of all its chaos.

The man had finally reached the end of his mental journey. Or so he thought... Suddenly, new images appeared unprompted in his mind: A man with a shaved head, a merciless confrontation, yet another defeat... What did it mean? He had to marshal his thoughts, he had he know!

A pain like no other struck him down. His brain almost shut down. He tried to hold on to his memories, but to no avail. He felt himself slipping into an abyss... Only a few muffled sounds still reached him, a conversation that he no longer was able to understand...

"He was about to wake up," said the First Speaker. "His spirit is strong, stronger than any being I have ever controlled in the past."

"What you caught in your psychic net is a titan," said the Second Speaker. "Not even your considerable mental powers can keep him in thrall for long."

"I know that! That's why I called you. You have the means to subjugate him permanently."

"Yes. The Mask of Amon will make him your slave."

The man felt an object being placed against his face. Then the darkness took over, and he was no more.

CHAPTER I
Baptism of Fire

Javier Acosta clung to his rifle as the troop transport vehicle carrying him bounced on the road. A quick glance at the other passengers confirmed that his eleven comrades were as nervous as he was. Despite the dim light, each soldier was staring at his companions, as if looking for courage in their numbers. They could hear the explosions outside, which the driver had so far managed to avoid, and feel the jolts of the truck.

Javier, like his comrades, was an elite soldier. He had enlisted in the U.S. Army at eighteen to escape the squalid ghettos of Los Angeles, where his only choice had been joining a gang or a life of poverty. A disciplined and efficient Marine, praised by his superiors, he had already fought in Iraq and Afghanistan. At some point, he had been noticed by C.L.A.S.H.[5] the U.N.-sponsored international anti-terrorist agency and, after an internship among the organization's troops, had become an active member of their military wing, soldiers sent to the front lines of extraordinary conflicts often involving superhuman and extraterrestrial threats.

The heavy silence in the truck was broken by Captain Alistair Wood, an Englishman whose rough manners contrasted with his posh accent. The officer pointed to the screen on the back of the driver's cabin on which various information was beginning to appear.

---

[5] Consortium for Law-Enforcement Action for the Security of Humanity.

"Look here, boys," he said in a clear and strong voice. "Here's the situation as we know it: this morning at ten-zero-zero—about half-an-hour ago—several unidentified airships materialized over Manhattan in a perimeter ranging roughly from Central Park to the East River and from 65th to 92nd Street. Without warning, the intruders began bombing civilians and landing troops…"

Wood scrolled through the news images on the screen by clicking on a remote control. The soldiers concentrated, studying the streamlined shapes of the alien vessels, spitting rays on the city below. The next image showed the invaders: reptilian creatures, looking like alligators walking on two feet, powerfully built and armed with sophisticated rifles.

"At present, we know neither the objective nor the plan of the invaders," Wood continued. "However, we have been able to identify them because they've attacked Earth before: they are the Xans, a fierce reptilian race from another dimension, usually employed as mercenaries. They're extremely dangerous, even when disarmed."

The screen now displayed precise diagrams of the attackers, their ships and their weapons, and various biological records. The soldiers soaked up all this, which might soon make the difference between life and death.

"Right now, we're the only ones on site, except for a handful of brave NYPD officers and four National Guards helicopter. The *Leviathan*[6] is too far from New York to be of help right now, and the U.S. Army is mobilizing but won't be able to intervene for at least another half-hour—plenty of time for those green-skinned bastards to do a lot of damage to the Big Apple! And, of

---

[6] C.L.A.S.H.'s flying fortress.

course, none of those damn superheroes are around when we need them!"

The soldiers looked at each other. All had hoped for the support of at least some superhumans in this battle— the Bronze Gladiator, the Hexagon Group... The tension rose inside the armored truck.

"The plan is by no means to repel this invasion," the captain continued. "Our one and only objective is to secure the perimeter in order to allow the civilian population to evacuate. The NYPD have already begun. We're here to provide them with logistics and tech support while waiting for reinforcements to arrive. In short, we are saving time and lives."

A bump more pronounced than the others caused the vehicle to jump, and each soldier found himself almost slumped over his comrade on the left. Javier grabbed the safety strap. His heart started beating faster. The vehicle came to a halt. They had arrived!

Captain Wood rushed to the rear and pushed the big red button that opened the exit hatch. The rear of the transport unfolded and the light of a warm New York day crept into the cabin.

"Go, go, go!" shouted the officer as the soldiers disembarked. Javier, who was at the far end of the truck, was the last to go out. The other soldiers had already deployed according to procedure, covering themselves on every side with the typical efficiency of C.L.A.S.H.'s elite troops, a choreography mixed with a martial aesthetic.

Javier took his spot without even thinking about it, his body following a training that he had repeated a thousand times. With his pulse rifle pointed in front of him, he could see the chaos that had engulfed this section of Manhattan, In the sky, half a dozen alien ships stood still, spraying the ground with iridescent rays. On the ground, cars were burning everywhere. One could hear both screams of terror and war-like vociferous shouts in a sibilant alien tongue. Dark smoke rose between the buildings which all sported broken windows and cracked walls.

Watching this ghastly spectacle, Javier felt a cold rage grip his heart; he saw that all his comrades were stiffening. In the adjacent streets, two other troop transports took up positions and disembarked their occupants. A distant roar indicated the arrival of the National Guard's helicopter gunships, armed with enough fire power to shoot down the alien ships.

Suddenly, a squad of Xan warriors came within sight of Javier's unit. The two formations paused, as if frozen by surprise. Then, the guns began to talk.

Five heavily armed soldiers ran for cover, protected by the fire of their comrades guarding their position from the rear. Javier joined them almost without thinking, his reflexes honed by years of training and experience. Diving behind the wreckage of a truck, he felt, more than he saw, a laser bolt brush past him. He didn't even have time to catch his breath; with a quick motion, he stood up and took aim at the Xans. His machine gun crackled in unison with those of his comrades. Heavy fire drove the aliens away, but without causing them much damage.

The soldiers secured the area, inspecting every corner of each alleyway. From where he stood, Javier could see that the other squads were doing the same thing, establishing a safe perimeter.

Captain Wood joined the other officers before issuing his instructions over the radio:

"Soldiers!" Javier's earpiece spat out. "We're going to follow an inverted triangle progression. You will take the southern flank while Captain Hung's unit will take the north. Captain Delpierre's unit will stay in reserve here. You have your orders! Good luck, gentlemen!"

Javier and his comrades obeyed immediately. After gathering with military speed, they advanced south of the attack perimeter silently, their jaws clenched in anger and apprehension.

They moved slowly, as each junction could conceal an ambush and needed to be approached with great caution. All the civilians they encountered were directed towards the rear. It was often difficult for the soldiers to make themselves understood and obeyed. In fact, many residents refused to leave their buildings, hoping to be safe there from the scourge descending upon their city. But the squad could not linger long to convince them. They merely nodded and moved on.

Javier was appointed as a scout by Sergeant Daek, a Korean built like a rugby player. Quick and observant, he was ideally suited for that task. He was examining a dead end when he detected some abnormal activity: the sounds of heavy footsteps on metal.

He looked up and spotted a half dozen Xans coming down a fire escape.

Laser rays started raining down on him and he leapt to take shelter behind a large dumpster. Grabbing his transmitter, he warned his comrades.

"Guys, Gators at three o'clock!" he shouted, trying to be heard over the sound. "I repeat..."

"Copy that, Acosta. Standing by."

From his shelter at the far end of the alley, Javier saw the Xans spread out into the adjacent avenue where they were greeted by heavy fire. The young soldier saw the power of the aliens: several were hit, but barely registered the shots. Their thick scales were a natural armor that protected them better than any bulletproof vest, even against C.L.A.S.H.'s advanced weaponry. Their laser guns, on the other hand, spat deadly fire that caused much damage to their human foes.

Clenching his teeth, the soldier tried to get out of the alley, but two Xans were guarding the backs of their comrades and a barrage of laser fire forced Javier to cower behind his precarious shelter. He decided to pull the pin out of a grenade, but instead of throwing it and thus becoming a target, he sent it rolling under the dumpster with just enough force to get it to the feet of the two aliens. The ensuing explosion was amplified by the narrowness of the alley and Javier thrown backwards by the blast. The container behind which he hid crashed into him. With his legs trapped, he still saw his squad taking advantage of the opportunity he had created: blown away by the grenade, the Xans were shot down quickly and mercilessly.

Two soldiers—Jones, a sturdy black man, and Wendell, a Texan with a thick Southern drawl—walked into the alley and pulled Javier out of harm's way. They tipped the dumpster to the side and the young Latino boy quickly got up, only to find that the pain in his ankle forced him to limp. He winced and smothered an expletive; this was no time to be hurt.

"Are you all right, Acosta?" Sergeant Daek asked from the avenue.

"Could be better, but I'm not complaining, sergeant!" replied Javier, leaning on one leg. He then turned to Jones. "What are our losses?" he asked.

"They got Lanier and Greenberg," replied the other without letting his emotions transpire. "The Doc's hurt too, but that won't stop him from taking a look at your leg."

"My leg's OK!" protested the soldier before stumbling and being caught in extremis by Wendell.

"Sure looks OK to me!" joked the Texan, continuing to support him. "We'll take you to him anyway, just in case."

Suddenly, a thunderous noise tore the Heavens apart. Javier and his two companions raised their heads, imitated by their comrades in the street. Two helicopters flew over them roaring. The sound of heavy machine guns mingled with that of the blades as the two attack vehicles set out to attack the Xans' ships.

The bullets having no visible effect, the helicopters switched to missiles, their white trails drawing curly arabesques against the blue of the sky. Again, it was a failure: the alien ships were protected by powerful force fields that kept the explosions at bay.

The helicopters made a wide turn to attack again and flew back over Javier's squad. Just then, they were struck by a powerful energy beam from the nearest Xan vessel.

For Javier, the scene seemed to take place in slow motion. The two copters exploded like overripe fruit and debris began to rain all over the city block. The bulk of the copters, burnt out but still in one piece, fell with a strange slowness along with the twisted blades of the propellers. As if in a nightmare, Javier thought that one of the wrecks was going to fall right on top of him, but that was only an optical illusion. The fireball that had become the cockpit crashed into the next street, where the rest of his squad was stood.

A final explosion shook the surrounding area and the three soldiers threw themselves to the ground.

Javier straightened up, a scream stuck in his throat. He realized that he had lost consciousness for a brief moment; a pain in the back of his head indicated that he must have been knocked out by a bit of shrapnel. He was lucky it had not been more serious.

Jones and Wendell also stood up, looking dazed. Thick grey smoke filled the block and restricted their view. Despite the anguish that gripped him, Javier let his reflexes take over. Rifle pointed in front of him, he took measured steps towards the avenue, trying to ignore the pain from his injured ankle.

After watching the perimeter through the dust and the burning wreckage, he signaled to his comrades to join him. The three of them slung their weapons over their shoulders and rushed to the crash site. The sight that awaited them froze the blood in their veins despite all their combat training.

Their squad had been annihilated. Caught in the explosion of the crashing helicopter, the soldiers hadn't had a chance. A quick tour of the perimeter confirmed their worst fears: no survivors. Scattered body parts littered the devastated street. Javier, Jones and Wendell collected tags whenever possible. In the distance, they heard more explosions, but no more helicopters flew overhead.

"What do we do now?" Wendell asked.

"We have our orders," Javier replied grabbing his radio. "PFC Acosta base. PFC Acosta to base. Do you read me?"

Only static answered him. After several attempts, he gave up and faced the unpleasant facts.

"We're alone," he said.

"So, what do we do next?" Wendell repeated.

Jones took a machine gun under each arm.

"We kill each and every one of these sons of bitches," he said with boiling rage.

Javier nodded and retrieved several grenades.

"As far as we know, we're on our own," he stated. We're going to follow our original orders: get as many civilians to safety as possible, and as a bonus, destroy as many of those damn gators as possible."

The three soldiers started moving towards the central area of the attack with determined steps.

The entrance to a Subway station was the scene of a bizarre spectacle. Police officers, whose cars were parked across the street to protect the entrance, tried as best as they could to channel the flow of refugees. The epicenter of the invasion was only a block or two away, as evidenced by the shouting, the screams and the sound of gunfire. Panicked civilians were jostling each other at the risk of injuring themselves.

Javier and his two comrades quickly reached the Subway entrance, identified themselves and asked for a status report. A potbellied NYPD officer with a sweat-soaked moustache answered them.

"Well, we don't know much. We did run into a few C.L.A.S.H. men, but they all rushed into combat, leaving us in charge of civilian evacuations. We hope they're holding on over there because there's still a lot of people to be moved here!"

Javier took a look around and realized that the area was too open—an intersection between two wide avenues, with a Subway entrance on either side. An attack by the Xans would result in a massacre...

"Officer, we need to reinforce the perimeter," he said. "Park your cars across the streets and position two men behind each. Make sure all the angles are covered."

The policeman did not hesitate for a moment and began to relay the orders on his radio. Several New Yorkers took a stunned look at Javier's dark blue uniform, very different from that of their own armed forces.

In less than five minutes, the intersection was fortified as he had requested. It wasn't much, but in the end, it would have to suffice.

It was Jones who sounded the alarm. About ten Xans came out from the site of the attack. Javier decided that they had to buy the NYPD men some time. He signaled to the two policemen guarding the entrance to the Subway to speed up things, but the crowd, seeing the nightmarish creatures coming, panicked and quickly created chaos.

Jones came out of his dugout, a machine gun under each arm, and shouted his hatred as he fired wildly at the Xans. His fire mowed down several aliens, and that was the signal for the battle to begin.

The policemen took aim with their sawed-off rifles and fired. Wendell positioned himself to cover Jones and aimed at each of his targets with a professional sharpshooter's eye. Each of his shots hit the chink in the aliens' armored hides and killed them on the spot. But more Xans arrived, drawn by the sounds of the battle, and they began to overwhelm the city defenders. Despite their obvious lack of discipline, and the humans' steady fire, they advanced inexorably and gained a clear advantage; their physical strength and superior weaponry made them almost impossible to beat.

Horrified, Javier saw several policemen fall after being struck by enemy lasers. These men had shown a rare courage and he swore it would not be in vain. Joining his two comrades, he broke through the ranks of the

Xans, hoping to create enough confusion to give time for the civilians to flee into the neighboring streets.

A policeman used his car like a battering ram and drove towards the aliens. He mowed down several of them before a laser bolt hit his chest. The uncontrolled vehicle crashed into a fire hydrant and soon water started raining all over the intersection.

Javier, Jones and Wendell retreated into an alleyway littered with debris—a mediocre shelter, at best. The young soldier sowed their path with grenades to draw the Xans away from the civilians. The aliens went in pursuit, hoping to finish what must have seemed to them like some futile opposition. Jones stood at the entrance to the alleyway and emptied his magazines with a loud shout.

"You, bastards!"

The big man was hit from all sides by laser bolts but remained standing as long as possible. When his machine guns rattled empty, he finally collapsed, face down on the ground. Javier and Wendell threw away their now useless rifles, drew their automatic pistols—nigh useless weapons in the face of such opponents—unloading them on their opponents. With desperation, Javier saw a battalion of Xans scurrying after the population, sowing corpses amidst cries of terror.

After Wendell fell, Javier didn't know what else to do. There was only one Xan left in front of him, and the soldier watched with ferocious pleasure as the bodies of a dozen of these accursed aliens strewed the ground in front of him. The soldier took his survival knife out of its case and brandished it in front of him.

"Come on, you f*** gator..."

The Xan observed him for a moment and a glimmer of amusement passed through his eyes. He threw his rifle to the side and walked towards the human who was challenging him.

Javier took the time to scrutinize the alien, a cold sweat running down his back. The Xan was almost seven feet high and his muscular body was completely naked. Its crocodile-like face lay directly on a large torso, further accentuating the impression of raw power it radiated. Its long mouth was lined with tapering fangs, while its fingers all ended in sharp claws. He was a monster from mankind's worst nightmares.

Yielding to a primitive fear from the depths of time, Javier took a step back. He felt like vomiting and started to shake. Then he saw over the creature's shoulder the death and destruction wrought by his comrades. His fear quickly turned to rage, and an animal cry came out of his throat. He leapt to the attack, his blade pointing toward the heart of his opponent.

The Xan simply swung his thick arm to intercept his attacker, but Javier feinted and aimed lower. His knife slipped on the alien's thigh, barely cutting through the scales. Undeterred, he struck again with the same gesture, this time taking advantage of the fact that he was almost behind his opponent.

The blade arched and plunged into the back of the Xan's knee. This time, the monster gave a cry of pain and kicked back to get rid of his foe. Hit in the chest, Javier was thrown out of the alley but managed to roll out of reach.

Breathlessly, the soldier got back on his feet as best he could. His vision blurred for a moment and a dull pain in his chest made him realize that he likely had several broken ribs.

The Xan advanced towards him with a determined but cautious step. Javier flashed a defiant smile.

"So, big guy, not so sure about me, now?"

The alien responded with a series of croaks and hisses before diving at the human. Surprised by his speed, Javier was swept away by a blow to the shoulder and cried out in pain.

The Xan brutally pinned him to the ground and crushed him under its weight. His large scaly hands grabbed Javier's throat and began to squeeze.

While being asphyxiated, the soldier thought he could see a glimmer of amusement in the monster's eyes. This aroused his anger again. He might die here, but he would take the bastard to Hell with him!

Javier reached out with his arm and stuck his thumb into the monster's eye. That was enough to make him loosen, if only very slightly, his crushing embrace. That was all the soldier needed. He struck the underside of the Xan's mouth with his blade—a smooth area, poorly protected by the scales.

The knife went in, but not deep enough, and the alien resumed his strangulation with redoubled vigor. Javier knotted every muscle in his neck to hold on as long as he could—if only for a few more seconds. His hand struck again and again to widen the wound caused by his knife.

Thick, disgusting blood flowed into his mouth as the Xan's arms gradually weakened. At that moment, nothing else existed for Javier but the monster crushing his throat. It was a struggle of two mighty wills, each as inflexible as the other.

Finally, the alien threw itself back, its mouth and eyes dripping with a blackish blood. Kneeling over the soldier, the Xan cried out in pain and rage. Javier realized that this would be his only chance: he unhooked a grenade from his belt and pushed it into his enemy's oversized mouth before struggling to crawl as far as he could.

The Xan appeared surprised and tried to extract the metal sphere from his throat, but he was too late. The blast tore his head off and split his chest in two; it also sent Javier flying five yards away and he had to make a superhuman effort not to faint.

Lying on his back, Javier felt his strength abandon him. The surrounding silence told him that the intersection was now deserted; the policemen were probably all dead and the Xans free to continue their work of destruction.

A feeling of despair gripped his heart; guilt for not having fulfilled his duty to the end.

Suddenly, he heard a loud crash that shook all the surrounding buildings; he recognized it as a supersonic boom.

Scanning the skies, he soon spotted the unmistakable silhouette of the world's most powerful fighter plane: the Hexajet!

Javier felt a new hope in his heart. The Hexagon Group was finally here—the most powerful superheroes on Earth!

With what little strength he had left, he made a fist towards the plane.

"Kick their asses, boys!" he shouted.

Then Javier Acosta lost consciousness, lying among the corpses and burnt carcasses.

CHAPTER II
The Battle of New York

A heavy silence reigned inside the cockpit of the Hexajet. The six members of Hexagon were huddling together in a space that was too narrow for all of them. They beheld the awful spectacle of desolation that this section of New York had become.

The sky above the Big Apple was still overflown by the Xan cruisers. The supersonic plane turned around and began deploying its weapon systems. His eyes filled with anger, Dominik Nero, a.k.a. the Dark Flyer, sat at the controls, his hands clenched on the controls, his knuckles whitening under the strain.

At his side, the magnificent Black Lys, dressed in her dark blue and ebony suit, put her hand on his shoulder, as if to calm him down. Sitting in the co-pilot's seat, Rakar analyzed the situation from a military standpoint. A former US Marine, he knew how to keep a cool head even in the direst circumstances. Behind him, the imposing Blackie Sullivan remained indecipherable; his all-black uniform echoed the city's mourning in this tragic hour.

In the back, the Mysterious Archer was meticulously checking his weapons, ready for battle. Finally, Ra, the newest and most powerful member of the Group, was elbowing his way to evaluate the extent of the threat posed by the alien invaders.

No one talked. They had just returned from the West Coast where a major earthquake had wreaked havoc. The six heroes had done their best to help the relief effort and save as many lives as possible before returning to their New York headquarters. As they approached the city, they had picked up numerous distress calls. None of the team members could have imagined such a tragedy. They felt guilty that they had not been there to counter the attack from its very beginning. But now, that feeling had been replaced by the acute awareness of the work to be done.

Black Lys called up an image on a touch-screen monitor, which she turned to show her teammates.

"As the only original member here, I have identified these attackers because I've fought them before," she said. "They're the Xans, an alien race from the Negative Universe of Zhud with reptilian physiology. They have attacked Earth in the past; they usually serve Aster's arch-enemy, the tyrant Melanos—the reason behind the founding of Hexagon."

The other five Hexagoneers studied took the images scrolling down the screen.

"They're tough, but we've seen worse. Rakar," she added Lys, turning toward the young Lakota, "what is your evaluation of their plan of attack?"

Rakar hesitated for a moment, leaning over another monitor that was tracking the invaders' progress through the city.

"That's the trouble, Lys," he finally said. "I don't see any pattern here. It's a massive assault, but one without any rhyme or reason."

"I agree," Fred Sullivan said, pointing to the data. "They seem to have no other purpose than to wreak havoc."

Black Lys—a.k.a. Cendrine de Mérignan—seemed baffled for a second. She bit her lower lip in reflection.

"What do we do then?" asked the Dark Flyer, still tense in his seat.

The silver-haired Frenchwoman sighed and closed her eyes. When she opened them again, an unearthly glow lit up her purple eyes.

"Well, let's keep it simple, too! Dominik and Fred, shoot down their ships; Rakar and Ra, neutralize their ground forces; the Archer and I will try to organize what remains of law enforcement. We'll remain in telepathic contact throughout."

Each member nodded. Cendrine was an exceptional leader and her comrades had learned to trust her. She had led them to victory more than once, in much more desperate situations. Dominik Nero pressed a button and a door opened on the side of the Hexajet; a thin force field preventing decompression inside.

The heroes rushed out without a moment's hesitation, throwing themselves into the void one after the other. Before jumping, Lys turned to the Dark Flyer.

"Dominik, notify C.L.A.S.H. and the Pentagon that we're stepping in. Ask them to contact me asap so that we can coordinate our efforts in the field."

Then she jumped out—and into battle.

The five Hexagoneers fell in free fall for a moment before being engulfed inside a globe of light. Their descent gradually slowed down until they approached the city below. This was the work of Ra, a.k.a. Ben Leonard, endowed with the powerful psionic powers of the legendary Sun God of the Egyptian pantheon.

The heroes soon found themselves standing on top of a Midtown skyscraper. This was the moment Blackie Sullivan chose to call upon the power of the Soul of Levan—the hereditary power of his proud lineage. This ancient and mysterious force gave him mastery over dark matter, a cosmic element essential to the cohesion of the universe. That gift made him one of the most powerful superhumans on Earth.

Blackie Sullivan's body was soon enveloped by a dark radiance that concealed his features and transformed him into a figure crackling with dark matter energy. His control of that substance enabled him to defy gravity. He freed himself from Ra's psychic globe and headed towards the Xan ships.

"I'm not going to try to be gentle," he warned his comrades. "Lys, Archer, try to get everyone to safety. I'm not sure I can prevent falling debris when I blow their god damn ships to pieces."

Without waiting for an answer, Fred Sullivan went off to fight in the skies. Black Lys smiled: once a supervillain and their mortal enemy, Blackie had turned into a major asset for Hexagon, but his old ways had barely softened. She almost pitied the Xans who would face him at the height of his power.

"Cendrine, where do you want me to drop you off?" Ra asked.

Lys cast an inquiring glance at the Mysterious Archer. The latter was scanning the surrounding neighborhoods, subjecting the situation on the ground to his superhuman gift of environmental analysis. His brain assimilated all the information and examined every eventuality to arrive at the best possible strategic decision.

"Drop us on that big avenue there, north of the perimeter," he suggested without a moment's hesitation. "That's where we'll have the best chance of joining the Army and cutting off the Xans' advance."

Ra nodded and, with a mere thought, dispatched the Black Lys and the Mysterious Archer to that very spot. Then he turned towards Rakar and asked:

"And what is our strategy?"

"Look over there," replied the Lakota warrior. "From that rooftop, a small group of Xans is covering a wide area. I'll take care of them and help make rescue efforts safer. You, you'll be most useful in the streets. Go down to ground level and eliminate all the enemy patrols you come across."

"Will do."

Ra levitated to a point located just above the roof of the building occupied by the Xans and dropped his comrade. As he fell, Rakar pulled out his tomahawk and cutlass, his two favorite weapons, engraved with powerful Lakota spells. The warrior landed straight upon one of the Xans and fell him with his full weight. The alien screamed out as much in surprise as in pain, alerting the others.

Without giving him time to recover from the shock, Rakar smashed his skull with his tomahawk, striking as ruthlessly as his famous ancestor. The Xan collapsed, killed instantly, as the hero rolled over to cushion his fall.

Rising up, Rakar assessed the situation: the other four aliens surrounding him had raised their laser guns to smite him down. With a swift and sure movement, he threw his cutlass and pierced the heart of one of his opponents. The magic blade was barely slowed down by the Xan's thick scales and reached his heart without deviating from its trajectory.

Energy bolts flashed around the Lakota, who positioned himself to prevent the other Xans from aiming at him without risking touching each other. Indeed, one of the aliens had just accidentally shot down one of his comrades.

There were only two Xans left. The first one uttered a wild cry and rushed to attack, the butt of his weapon raised. Rakar dodged him with ease and hit the Xan's knee with his tomahawk, breaking the bone. As the reptilian fell to his knees, flapping his arms, the Hexagoneer turned around and struck a second powerful blow to the back of his skull. The creature fell to the ground, dead.

The last Xan now hesitated. This seemingly frail human had eliminated four of his brothers in no time and without a scratch. Rakar stood still in front of him, at a cautious distance. The alien finally raised his weapon, but the warrior reacted immediately. With a kick, he threw his last victim's laser rifle into the air and grabbed it before throwing himself to the ground and firing.

The Xan's ray narrowly missed the Hexagoneer, but he himself hit his target, shooting down his last opponent.

The confrontation had lasted less than a minute. Ra, who had been watching from above, was speechless. He had only been a member of Hexagon for a few weeks and had learned to value his teammates; this attack on New York was the first combat mission he had ever been on. He had come to recognize Blackie Sullivan's brute force and raw power, or the technological wizardry of the Dark Flyer, but he never had thought that Rakar, seemingly without superhuman powers, could be so deadly. He obviously had underestimated him.

He waved his hand to his teammate and levitated down to street level. He, too, had his share of work to do.

Rakar (whose civilian name was Francis White River) watched Ra move away. The newest member of

Hexagon was a young blond man, dressed in a golden uniform with a black sun on his chest. He had reported for duty a few weeks ago, after Kathryn Sullivan, a.k.a. Plasma, had gone on maternity leave.

Kathryn was Rakar's girlfriend and was pregnant with twins, a condition somewhat incompatible with her superheroic activities. The team had had to work hard to convince the young woman to take a break; she was just as stubborn as her late father, Jeff, but in the end, had relented. She had returned to live with her mother, Mary, in Colorado, and the two women took care of each other, even though Kathryn insisted on returning occasionally to New York for a day or two to stay abreast of Hexagon's business.

As for Douglas, Jeff and Fred's youngest brother and Kathryn's uncle, he had returned from Africa, where he ran a medical clinic, to be with his niece, just in case...

After Plasma's departure, Hexagon had not remained incomplete for long. For reasons beyond Rakar's understanding, the team always strove to have had six active members. Ra, who had been in C.L.A.S.H.'s diamond files[7] for a while, had been approached and recruited only a few days after Kathryn's departure.

The young man had not hesitated to reveal his true identity in order to establish a bond of trust: his name was Ben Leonard and he was a journalist specialized in ancient history and archaeology. He possessed impressive psionic powers, including telepathy and telekinesis. Of Franco-American origin, he had however chosen Ra as his code name, in homage to the Egyptian sun god.

---

[7] Files about superpowered individuals residing on Earth.

Black Lys had conducted a further background check on him with the help of Mister Song of C.L.A.S.H. but had found nothing suspicious. In fact, even C.L.A.S.H. had very little information on the amazing Mr. Leonard, and some of what they had was barely believable.

This had not failed to arouse a little suspicion in some of the Group. Dominik Nero, for instance, remained wary and skeptical, but Rakar had known from the start that the young superhero was the perfect archetype necessary to replace Plasma. If the young woman was the Mistress of Fire, Ben Leonard was the Master of the Sun. On the advice of the Lakota, Hexagon had accepted Ra into their ranks.

During the previous weeks, the Group had not faced any major threats. In fact, since their battle with Ghool[8] that had nearly wiped out all traces of civilization on Earth, Hexagon had essentially performed humanitarian missions. It almost seemed as if their recent recruitment of Blackie Sullivan had cooled the desires of their various archenemies and other evildoers to tackle them. During this period of relative calm, Ra had proved to be a very effective hero and showed a level of experience that was astonishing for a relative beginner. But now, this violent assault by the Xans would test him in a real combat situation. Rakar hoped that he would do as well as he had done in their previous operations.

After retrieving his cutlass, Francis White River knelt by the body of the Xan with the pierced heart. He dipped two fingers in the alien's viscous blood and drew ancient patterns on his face, mystical war paintings, essential elements of the spell he was about to cast. He

---

[8] See *Hexagon: Dark Matter*.

stood up and began to recite an incantation in the secret tongue of the Lakota shamans.

Suddenly, a sound made him turn around; several aliens had just appeared showed up the fire escape—probably sent to replace those he had slain. When they saw the slaughter of their brethren, the Xans shouted in rage and hurled threats at the human they correctly held responsible for the massacre.

With a ferocious smile, Rakar turned and ran to the edge of the building. The laser bolts crackled around him but none reached him. The Hexagoneer leapt up and landed on the roof of the next building, several stories below. The aliens immediately chased him. Rakar ran and jumped from one building to another, sometimes changing direction abruptly, going up and down using every trick he knew. The warrior knew exactly where he was going, and the aliens were forced to follow him.

Rakar had a keen awareness of what he was doing, but the Xans were powerfully built, and they were gradually gaining ground. The shots were getting dangerously close and, more than once, the young hero had to rely on his instincts to save his life. Yet, despite the risks, he did not deviate once from his intended path.

That path brought him back after fifteen minutes of intense pursuit to the roof of the first building, the one where Ra had dropped him. Then, at last, Rakar stopped and turned to face his pursuers.

The Xans showed no sign of fatigue, but their anger was very real. The Lakota uttered a last word of power: the final invocation of his spell.

Instantly, the entire city block which he had just circled about in his mad dash, began to glow blue. The aliens then began an almost comical choreography: as if they had lost control of their limbs, they bumped into each other and, in the confusion, two of them fell to the bottom of the building.

With weapons in hand, the Hexagoneer walked quietly towards his opponents, now unable to fire at him with their laser guns. He mercilessly finished them off one by one before breathing a long sigh of relief.

Rakar sat to regain his strength.

"This is Rakar," he thought projected using the psychic channel that Ra had created between the Hexagoneers. *"I have just cast a spell of confusion on an entire city block. It affects only the Xans and reverses their perceptions. In effect, in this zone, they are unable to tell right from left. Usher them toward my position, and they'll become easy targets."*

"Well done, Francis," replied Lys in the same manner. *"I'll pass the word to the forces on the ground."*

Rakar got up and walked down the fire escape that led to the bottom of the building. His work wasn't finished.

Blackie Sullivan was gloating. Since he had inherited the Soul of Levan and all the power that came with it, he had fought only one worthy battle, the one against the Mad Fomore, Ghool. After that, the Group had not had to solve any major crisis. Even though Blackie was now a hero, he hadn't lost his taste for battle, especially now that he had power beyond compare.

He was well aware that the devastation in New York and the civilian casualties were a tragedy, but he was barely moved by it. The world was a dangerous place and Hexagon could not be everywhere at once. All that mattered now was to end the threat of the Xans as soon as possible—and he was going to enjoy himself during this confrontation.

Fred Sullivan's black-clad silhouette was flying at high speed towards one of the alien starships. The crew must have spotted him because shots were fired in his direction. He avoided them, at first with ease, then decided to show the Xans the full extent of his powers.

He stood still in the sky, his arms outstretched in a defiant posture. The ship pointed all its cannons at him and fired a flurry of iridescent rays. They crashed into Blackie Sullivan but became lost in the aura of darkness surrounding his body. The master of dark matter didn't even shudder under the impact. On the contrary, he laughed.

"Is that all you have?" he shouted. "It won't be enough!"

"Are you having a good time?" Dominik Nero asked him, telepathically.

"I'm just getting started. Are you going to put on your armor and join the party?" Blackie replied.

"I don't have to. The entire Hexajet is my armor."

Still seated at the controls of the supersonic, the Dark Flyer entered a series of instructions, then spoke the word "process" aloud for voiceprint recognition.

Immediately, thin metal tentacles emerged from the back of his seat and affixed themselves to his head, sending nanotech filaments connecting the machine to his neural network. A visor came down from the ceiling and lowered itself in front of his face. Dominik's body relaxed as his mind invaded every corner of the Hexajet. Man and machine had become one.

Blackie Sullivan saw the plane make a sharp turn to the right and execute a mock salute. It then went supersonic as it leapt towards the alien vessel. It was a streamlined ship with a pointed tip and a large vertical wing at the back—inelegant ship, but despite its mass, fast. Less fast, however, than the Hexajet when it used its nuclear engines.

The plane passed within a few inches of the Xan ship, almost grazing it, and the Dark Flyer used this opportunity to scan and analyze the enemy vessel. Data scrolled across his visor, warning him of the presence of a force field of high magnetic density. He smiled and mentally commanded the Hexajet to activate his latest addition to its weaponry.

Under the wings, two batteries deployed. Dominik fired. Hollow rods of hexagonium—an alloy he had created and which was the strongest metal on Earth—were ejected by a high-velocity electric wave. They whistled through the sky and went through the enemy ship's shield before tearing its armored hull in several places.

The Xan vessel was soon pierced through and through. It nosedived for a moment before a series of explosions surged through it, turning it into a massive ball of flames. Debris began to rain down, but the Hexajet soon reduced it to a fine dust with its targeted atomizing fire. The aircraft, guided by the prodigious mind of the Dark Flyer, ensured that no further damage was inflicted upon the hapless Big Apple.

"I wanted that ship," Blackie Sullivan complained.

"First come, first served!" replied Dominik Nero. *"Besides, there are five more ships for you to indulge yourself. And it looks like they've spotted us…"*

The other Xan vessels had left their stationary positions and were now heading towards the two heroes. To preserve their strategic advantage, Blackie Sullivan decided to strike first. Dark energy crackled around his fists. Extending his arms forward, he projected a thick beam of dark matter towards one of the alien vessels.

The beam crashed into the Xans' force field, but Blackie held firm and continued to pour energy upon the same spot. Sparks began to appear across the invisible surface of the shield and, suddenly, it collapsed under the density of the dark matter hammering it. Now unimpeded, the ebony beam first caused the vessel to explode before engulfing it inside a gravitational singularity, making it vanish.

"Not bad when it comes to cleaning up the mess," the Dark Flyer commented.

While dodging the fire from the four remaining enemy ships, Dominik felt a bead of sweat running down his face. Fred "Blackie" Sullivan had once been one of Hexagon's fiercest foes. With all this new power now at his disposal, what would happen if he decided to go back to his old ways... He chased the thought away; there were more pressing matters to deal with...

The Dark Flyer sneaked between two Xan vessels and sprayed them with nail gun fire—with little effect. The Xans tried to keep the Hexajet in their sights, but as they did so, they came dangerously close to each other. When they were positioned just as Dominik had anticipated, he launched another salvo of hexagonium rods. Once again, this seemingly primitive weapon made the Xans' superior technology look obsolete and struck a deadly blow to one of the cruisers.

Fatally damaged by the rods, it lost control of its flight and collided with the other ship, whose force field then burst like a soap bubble. The two spaceships became intertwined in a pandemonium of fire and metal and disintegrated. Once again, the Hexajet hunted down the debris to protect the city below.

"Fred," called Dominik, *"I'm on clean up duty here; can you take care of the other two?"*

"Love to."

Blackie Sullivan charged towards the remaining vessels, whose fire he easily deflected thanks to his aura of dark matter.

Meanwhile, Ra was levitating through the streets of Manhattan. His body was surrounded by a golden aura as bright as the sun, the visible manifestation of his psychic powers.

The hero was aware that this battle would solidify his place in Hexagon. He had already proven his abilities during the preceding weeks, but these crises had been humanitarian missions without great needs for superhuman powers.

Ben Leonard smiled at the thought that his teammates thought that he was a beginner, new to the superhero game. He had decided to keep them in the dark, even though he didn't want to lie to them... He would reveal his true nature in due course, when he felt like a full-fledged member. After all, he hadn't joined Hexagon by chance. He hoped that, when the time came, the world's most powerful heroes would help him fulfill his destiny... But first, he had to gain their trust and esteem, and this battle was a good place to start.

Lost in his thoughts, Ra didn't see the ambush waiting for him at an intersection blocked by the wrecks of several vehicles. The impact of the Xans' laser fire on his aura suddenly brought him back to reality. His psionic screen deflected most of it, but he still felt the full force of the enemy fire and grimaced. No wonder the humans were overwhelmed. The aliens had technologically superior weapons at their disposal.

Ra stopped his flight and confronted levitated the enemy squad facing him. The aliens fired again. Inside his psychic bubble, Ben was safe. With a wave of his hand, he lifted the still burning carcass of a car and, squeezing his fingers into an angry fist, reduced it to a crumpled ball of metal, which he then launched at high speed towards his foes. The improvised projectile scattered the Xans in an explosion of debris. Several aliens lay helpless, but others were already regrouping. Their sheer aggressivity appalled Ra, who brought them down by projecting a psychic wave that directly affected the pain centers of their brains.

Once the enemy had been neutralized, he took flight again to get a better overview of the situation. Floating near the top of a building, he saw an intense blue light rising from the block where he had left Rakar a moment earlier. He intercepted the Lakota's mental message to the rest of the Group and smiled. Decidedly, this shaman was more than resourceful!

Ra also saw smoke rising from another direction and turned his extrasensory perceptions that way. He caught the thoughts of Black Lys, who was leading a counteroffensive with a battalion of American soldiers. *Good for her!* he thought. This meant that it was his responsibility to secure the area between the two.

Ra expanded his telepathic probe to concentrate on the unique mental signature of the Xans. By doing so, he accurately mapped their positions. Then, with unwavering resolve in his eyes, he went into battle.

With her right eye bearing the famous birthmark that gave her her name, Black Lys fought like a she-devil on the front line. Her two energy blades roared through the air as she performed feints, sowing death among the Xans who were reckless enough to approach her. Her "swords" were known to slice through even the strongest metals, so they had no trouble piercing the scaly skin of the reptilian aliens. Plus their bio-energy absorbed the laser fire targeting them. Cendrine's prodigious dexterity allowed her to parry each shot with ease, as she was the world's best fencer, combining infallible technique with unparalleled tactics, two qualities that made her a whirlwind of death on such a battlefield.

At her side, the Mysterious Archer was equally effective in his own cold and methodical way. He shot arrow after arrow with a speed that the eye could barely see. He hit the bull's-eye every time, always choosing the right target. The last descendant of a long line of Finnish snipers, Jukka Häyhä was the very example of the perfect soldier recruited by the Brotherhood of Archers of Graxonia. There was an unrevealed connection between this mysterious organization and Hexagon. Since the group's foundation, there had always been a Mysterious Archer in its ranks, Jukka being the second to carry this title.

The two heroes paved the way for a counterattack by the U.S. Army. When Black Lys and the Archer had appeared before General Patterson, he hadn't hesitated to follow their advice; Hexagon's reputation was well known amongst the Military. The Xans had banded together to repel this massive assault, and there was now a fierce battle in the streets of middle-Manhattan. Around the two heroes, soldiers were eager to take on those invaders who had dared to attack their country. Although underequipped against the Xans, the men fought valiantly, inspired by the Hexagoneers' courage.

Rakar's actions had dictated the Army's objective: to push the aliens back to the block that the shaman had bewitched, where they would become disoriented. General Patterson had issued precise orders and his men were following the plan to the letter. The soldiers deployed in an arc that gradually directed the Xans' retreat toward the targeted area. Black Lys and the Archer did their best to eliminate as many aliens as possible and reduce human losses.

Suddenly, one of the ships in the sky exploded with a deafening roar. A clamor arose among the soldiers, which grew louder still as another cruiser seemed to collapse upon itself before disappearing. Cendrine smiled despite the fatigue that was beginning to weigh on her arms. She knew that Fred Sullivan and Dominik Nero were providing air cover, so the army didn't have to fear a bombardment.

"It's not over yet," said the Mysterious Archer whose eyes were scanning the sky.

No sooner had these words been spoken than two more alien ships were engulfed in a ball of fire, seemingly colliding with each other for no reason. Jukka allowed himself a little laugh.

"At least, they're having fun up there."

"Hey! We've got something to celebrate here too," replied Black Lys.

The Army had redoubled its efforts following the destruction of the alien vessels. The Xans were being driven back towards the bewitched block. Cendrine strengthened her resolve and leapt toward a small group of aliens who, sheltered behind a collapsed newsstand, hindered the advance of the soldiers. Her blades sliced through the guns pointed at her, then, after an elegant *salto*, she found herself in the midst of her enemies. Throwing away their now useless weapons, the Xans flexed their muscles and growled menacingly.

"So, which one of you is gonna ask me to the dance?" asked Black Lys jokingly.

One of the Xans threw himself at her, all claws out. She easily dodged the attack and swirled around to throw him off balance and slay him in a single movement. The lifeless body did not have time to touch the ground that Cendrine was already slipping between the massive arms of another alien, and in one devilishly smooth move, piercing his chest and drawing her blade back out of the massive body. She then stabbed the belly of another Xan and decapitated another. She knelt to avoid a treacherous claw and struck blindly backwards, killing her attacker. Finally, she leapt up to the crocodile-like mouth of her last foe and plunged her blade right inside his throat.

Now that the intersection had been cleared, the soldiers were able to resume their advance. More than one man whistled at the stunningly beautiful superheroine as they marched on.

The Mysterious Archer led the counterstrike. His speed rivaled that of the soldiers' machine guns, much to the men's astonishment. His arrows, fired at superhuman speed, hit the weakest point in the Xans' armor unfailingly. When his quiver became empty, the Archer separated his bow into two equal parts and straightened it with a flick of his wrist. Once its string was retracted, the bow turned into two long truncheons. Bending his legs, Jukka mowed down a Xan who was rushing at him. After the alien was down, he snapped his neck with a sharp blow.

The Archer then began a deadly dance, crushing foes and leaving in his wake a trail of stunned aliens that the soldiers could finish off easily. Galvanized by his courage, the men advanced at double their previous speed.

Fred "Blackie" Sullivan was clinging with all his might to the magnetic shield that protected the ship he had targeted. Because of sheer obdurateness, the master of dark matter had decided that he would destroy that ship with his bare hands. He pushed against the invisible shield, digging and clawing with his fingers, enveloped in a crackling bubble of dark energy. All his muscles hurt as he spread his hands, seeking to tear the force field apart. He could feel the energy bending before him, ready to give way... He kept struggling. The veins in his neck swelled under the titanic effort. Finally, the field opened in half with a thunderclap and Blackie was able to easily dissipate the last remnants of magnetic energy.

Now, there was no longer anything to protect the alien vessel, whose guns had already proved ineffective against the dark-clad hero. He clung to the ship's nose and used dark matter to increase his weight. With his density thus multiplied hundreds of times, Blackie Sullivan forced the ship to dive forward and steered it toward a row of evacuated buildings.

"Dominik, can you confirm that those buildings are empty?"

"Give me a second," replied the Dark Flyer, scanning the buildings. *"Er, yes, everyone appears to have been evacuated. But what about the damage..."*

But Blackie Sullivan continued his inexorable effort even as the alien ship tried to resist with all the might of its engines, but in vain. Dominik couldn't believe his eyes: Fred was crashing an alien ship right into a midtown office block—with his bare hands, to boot! But it was too late to stop him, and he already had his hands full with the last Xan ship.

The crash shook the whole town as the cruiser hit the building. The structure collapsed under the shock and tons of rubble fell onto the avenue below, drowning it into a cloud of dust. The ship was shaken by a series of explosions that broke it in several places and its scattered remnants ended up embedded in the facades of the buildings. The whole block now looked like a surrealist sculpture of gargantuan proportions.

Breathless, his muscles aching from the effort, Blackie Sullivan had no time to rest. The Hexajet was in trouble with the last ship. Dominik had used all his hexagonium tubes and was now forced to rely on conventional weapons alone; but they proved useless against the Xans' force field. Further, he was starting to suffer from a persistent headache. Controlling the plane via neuro-interface required much concentration...

"Dominik, don't sweat it, I'm just going to shoot him down," said Blackie. *"Be ready to pulverize the debris."*

"Roger that. Thank you, Fred!"

As he had done before, Blackie Sullivan created a tiny black hole within his hands and launched it towards the enemy vessel. The dark object flew past the magnetic shield and hit the Xan ship, piercing it from side to side. Taking advantage of that opening, the Hexajet fired all its missiles and finished the job. The last alien ship broke up and whatever debris remained, crashed into the already ravaged block below, thus ending the invaders' aerial threat.

"Well done, Fred!" enthused the Dark Flyer. *"Now, go and check what's happening on the ground. I have to disconnect from the Hexajet before my brain trickles out of my ears."*

Blackie Sullivan nodded and began his descent towards New York.

Ra had erected a telekinetic dome around a group of fleeing civilians to protect them from the Xans' merciless advance. Ben Leonard had seen too much death today—and had dealt his share of it as well, ruthlessly eliminating every alien squad he had encountered. Glowing with barely controlled rage, he levitated ten feet above the aliens, his fists clenched and his mind burning with repressed power.

As soon as a Xan raised his gun, he unleashed his psychic power. Then, a psionic wave as deadly as a tsunami hit the invaders. Despite their strength, they were swept away by the mental assault. Without giving them time to regroup, Ra lifted a car off the ground and slammed it over his opponents, crushing them mercilessly. But some Xans had anticipated the attack and threw themselves to the side. They fired back at Ben, who was hit by laser fire. Much of his energy had been employed to protect the civilians, so he couldn't deflect the attack. The rays penetrated his telekinetic aura and he screamed in pain as he fell to the ground.

His golden uniform was torn, but fortunately the injuries were only superficial—minor, but painful, burns. Ra had to keep a clear mind in order to maintain his concentration. Emboldened by the success of their attack, the Xans rushed forward and started to beat him savagely with their rifle butts.

Ben managed to blur their perceptions and thus prevented them from injuring him seriously. Then, he stood up and expanded his golden aura in order to force his attackers to retreat. He caught one of the aliens in his telekinetic grasp and threw him at one of his brethren with force. After that, he mentally lifted up the laser rifles left on the ground and pointed them at the remaining Xans. The rays of their own weapons finished them off.

Ra took the time to regain his full strength before heading towards the small group of humans he had rescued.

"Is everyone all right?" he asked, dropping his protective field.

A man wearing a bus driver's outfit stepped forward.

"Er, yes, I think so... Thank you," he replied.

"I was only doing my duty. But this isn't over yet. Head towards Central Park, Hexagon and the army are driving the aliens in the opposite direction. You should be safe there."

"Aren't you coming with us?"

"I can't, I'm sorry. I still have to take care of the ones left behind—and there are other people like you who need rescuing."

Ra used his mind powers subtly to instill courage in the minds of the New Yorkers who were facing him. He wore his most reassuring expression.

"Have no fear, you're safe now. I've cleared the area, so you're in no danger."

The civilians looked at each other and smiled, their will strengthened by the words of this young hero bright as the sun. They watched him in awe as he took off and soon vanished amongst the devastated buildings.

Rakar patrolled the streets of the perimeter he had created, easily getting rid of the few Xans who still remained. Walking cautiously, he came to a major intersection where a fierce battle had obviously taken place. The ground was littered with bodies, both human and alien. The Lakota warrior saw that some of the men wore the blue garb of C.L.A.S.H.'s rapid intervention troops; others were ordinary NYPD officers; all were heroes who had given their lives to protect the city's inhabitants.

A movement caught Rakar's attention. One of the men on the ground was still moving feebly. The Hexagoneer knelt down beside him, holding his head. He was a young C.L.A.S.H. agent of Hispanic origin. His neck was bruised and blue, making it difficult for him to breathe. Despite the fact that he was barely conscious, he managed to grab the hand of the shaman, who then saw the tattoo on the man's wrist, one worn proudly by members of the Marine Corps.

Compassion seized Rakar's heart and he quickly wove a spell of healing around the young agent. A wave of vitality swept through the Latino's body. He straightened up and took in a long breath of air.

"Are you all right?" Rakar inquired.

"Yes... I think so," replied the C.L.A.S.H. agent, clearing his throat. "I really thought that this time, the end had come."

"Can you get up?"

Leaning on Rakar, the young man managed to stand up. He then shook the hand of his savior.

"I'm Agent Javier Acosta, from the C.L.A.S.H. rapid intervention force," he introduced himself.

"Francis White River... better known as Rakar, from the Hexagon Group."

"I recognized you, sir," said Javier, his voice full of respect. "Luckily, you arrived just in time. The situation was... well, beyond our control."

"But you stood your ground. Thanks to you and your fellow agents, the majority of the civilian population could be evacuated. All we had to do, really, was to clean up after you guys. You have nothing to be ashamed of, Soldier. *Semper fi!*"

"Thank you, sir," said Acosta, replying to the traditional Marine salute in kind.

The Agent stepped back, looking sadly at the bodies of his companions. Suddenly, he spied a strange glow at the edge of his field of vision. He stiffened, but Rakar put him at ease, a hand on his shoulder.

"It's all right, he's one of us."

Ra came to land in front of the two men. His beleaguered look and the damage to his uniform indicated that he had been in a tough fight.

"I'm glad to see you're OK," said Rakar. "What's the situation like at your end?"

"I cleared the whole area from here to the positions held by the Army," replied Ben Leonard. "Black Lys and the Archer shouldn't encounter any more trouble."

Rakar couldn't repress an admiring whistle when he heard the news. Their new recruit had certainly done a good job.

"Good work," he said, congratulating him.

"Thank you." Ra suddenly raised his hand. "According to the telepathic echoes I'm picking up, the Army has just entered the perimeter of your spell. And our teammates up there have eliminated the aerial threat..."

"So you won, then?" Acosta asked.

"No, *we* won," Rakar corrected him. "C.L.A.S.H., the NYPD, the Army... All the heroes who fought together this day to save New York."

Ra sat down heavily on the pavement.

"In that case, I'll give myself permission to take a short break," he joked.

Blackie Sullivan chose this moment to land not far from them. He waved away the dark matter that still enveloped his body and approached his teammates without saying a word. Although he bore no stigma from the battle he had just fought, he, too, was exhausted, but pleased that he had been able to use his power to defuse the crisis.

The Hexajet flew overhead and stopped about forty feet above the ground. A tractor beam deposited Dominik Nero next to the other Hexagoneers. His short black hair was drenched in sweat and his nose was bleeding, but he smiled at his companions.

Finally, Black Lys and the Mysterious Archer emerged from a neighboring avenue, accompanied by a US Army squad. The soldiers, always on the lookout, surrounded the perimeter to secure it. From a light jeep, General Patterson issued some last minute orders before joining the six Hexagoneers.

"On behalf of the United States and the city of New York, I thank you for your invaluable assistance," he said.

"Much appreciated, but there truly is no need for thanks, General," replied Cendrine. "It is Hexagon's mission to lend its assistance when such tragic events occur. We only regret that we couldn't be here sooner."

"My men will take care of the last of these invaders—assuming there are any left. I know you must be tired, but firefighters from all over the state have been mobilized to search for survivors. With your uncanny abilities, you'd be a great help to them..."

"Of course, General! Understood, boys?" Cendrine said, turning toward her team. "There are still lives to be saved!"

Despite their extreme exhaustion, all the Hexagoneers answered present without hesitation.

CHAPTER III
Debriefing

The Hexagoneers were gathered in their conference room—only a few blocks away from the area attacked by the Xans. Now dressed in civilian clothes, they were all utterly exhausted. The alien assault had taken place the week before, and during the rest of that week, the heroes had mobilized with the rescue teams to locate survivors in the smoking ruins. It had been an exhausting job, especially mentally. Hundreds of New Yorkers had died, slaughtered by the aliens. Unfortunately, the Hexagoneers had found more corpses than survivors. Everyone was still haunted by the horrors of that past week.

In addition to the six currently active members, Kathryn "Plasma" Sullivan and Sweet were also present. Kathryn had returned as soon as the authorities had lifted their blockade of Manhattan in order to be with Rakar, the father of the children she was carrying. The two lovers had been able to spend several nights together, a welcome relief for the young Lakota shaman after such a harrowing week.

As for Sweet, she practically lived at Hexagon's midtown HQ, where she was the Group's expert computer scientist and technology genius, not forgetting the fact that she was also the Dark Flyer's girlfriend.

Despite their fatigue, the heroes were anxious to review what had happened. Despite their victory, the situation was still potentially serious and therefore required extreme vigilance. Many answers remained to be found.

As the team leader, Black Lys chaired the meeting. She projected satellite images of the Xan attack onto the holographic screen rising from the center of their conference table. This global viewpoint was supposed to help them to discern a reason behind the alien assault.

"I know we are all still very tired, but I thank you for being here," Cendrine began. "Last week, New York became the target of a large-scale attack by the Xans, a hostile extra-dimensional race we've fought before..."

The screen enlarges the aerial views of Manhattan and focused on the section the aliens had targeted.

"Curiously," Cendrine continued, "our HQ did not seem to be their objective. Their true purpose remains unknown for the moment. Rakar, you said you couldn't discern a pattern behind their attack. What about now? You've had a chance to look at the report from C.L.A.S.H. and the Army."

The Lakota shaman rubbed his eyes; many documents were spread out in front of him. Kathryn sat beside him and put her hand on his.

"No, nothing new, even when one looks at the satellite readings," replied Rakar. "If these bastards had a plan of attack, it didn't follow any pattern as far as I can tell. It was a mindless, massive assault, nothing else."

Fred Sullivan stood up and pointed at several dots on the holoscreen.

"If their goal had been a simple invasion, trying to create a beach head, their ships would have positioned themselves here and here. The ground troops would have cut off our supply routes here and here. Also, with six heavily armed ships, it would have been easy for the Xans to destroy our HQ, but they didn't even try."

Everyone remained thoughtful for a moment. The riddle posed by that unfathomable attack did not reassure them. It was never a good thing not to be able to figure out an enemy's motives.

"Archer, you often see things we don't," Black Lys said. "Maybe you can make some sense of this?"

The Finn put down the file he had been studying.

"No, not this time. I'm afraid I can't detect anything else," he replied with a hint of a Nordic accent. "The only notion I've come up with is that, as cataclysmic as it was, maybe that attack was just a diversion."

"That parallels my thinking," said Dominik Nero. "I asked C.L.A.S.H. to cast a wider net and look for any signs of unusual activity—extradimensional, extraterrestrial and extratemporal. As of yesterday, they haven't detected anything yet, but they remain on high alert. Their Samael orbital station has also been placed on red alert."

Ben Leonard coughed slightly to attract attention. As the newest member of Hexagon, he did not yet dare to speak up spontaneously at their meetings. With a gesture, Black Lys invited him to speak.

"We're all referring to this as an *alien* attack," he said, "but I was struck by one thing: look at this footage, these ships literally appeared out of nowhere. They certainly didn't come from outer space."

A short silence followed.

"This might indicate a new form of dimensional transfer," said Black Lys. "The Xans come from Aster's negative universe—Zhud. In the past, they have mostly been used as cannon fodder by Melanos..."

Cendrine realized that she was the only one in the room who had actually taken part in these nearly historical events. She as the last founding member of Hexagon who had actually fought Melanos and his reptilian allies alongside Aster and Pinky. The original Archer had gone, the fist Dark Flyer had retired, White Mask had quit and Jeff Sullivan was dead. Of the original team, only she remained.

"Melanos hasn't resurfaced in years," noted the Dark Flyer. "But in the past, his plans were more subtle, better thought out. I find it difficult to picture him as being behind this attack."

"It's still a lead we should pursue," Sweet broke in. "I took the liberty of searching the Hexadata for all the known locations of his bases and cross-reference it with any energy signature that might have originated from a Xan vessel..."

Though devoid of superhuman powers, Sweet was one of the brightest minds on Earth. That, coupled with her resourcefulness and sense of improvisation, made her a great asset to the Group. She pressed a key to display the results of her algorithm.

"Voilà!"

A rotating picture of the globe appeared with several dots of light on it.

"Why, that's amazing! Thank you Sweet," said Black Lys with a warm smile. "I agree it's unlikely that Melanos is involved, but that's all we have. Dominik and I will go and investigate these locations, if only to rule them out."

"I'll come too," Sweet said.

"It could be dangerous!" Dominik protested.

Sweet made a face and shrugged her shoulders in defiance.

"First, you said Melanos was not involved. Also, do you really expect me to not want to tour the secret lairs of an extradimensional tyrant? No way, big boy!"

The Dark Flyer raised his eyes. He knew he would never have the last word with his girlfriend. He was one of the few people in the world who could talk sense into her, but he didn't want to do this in front of his teammates...

"What about me? Am I expected to twiddle my thumbs in the meantime?" asked Fred Sullivan.

"Hum. Until we know more, Fred, I'd like you to stay in reserve here," replied Cendrine. "If New York or any other major metropolis is attacked, Hexagon must be able to respond quickly. No more being caught off guard like we were last week!"

Everyone agreed, and the meeting was over.

Black Lys, the Dark Flyer and Sweet went to the armory to equip themselves before leaving for South America to investigate the first of Melanos' old bases. The other members of Hexagon remained behind in the meeting room, either lost in their thoughts or too tired to talk.

Blackie Sullivan rose abruptly.

"I hate to have to wait like this!" he exclaimed. "If you're looking for me, I'll be blowing off steam in the training room."

Plasma smiled as she watched her uncle walk out of the room. What a contrast he offered with her father, the celebrated Man of Brass! Impulsive and daring, he hadn't mellowed much since joining Hexagon, even though he had left his dark past behind. The young woman wrapped her arms around Rakar's shoulders.

"As for you, my darling," she said in a playful tone, "you still need some R&R!"

Ra and the Mysterious Archer were left alone after the couple had left the room. Ben Leonard couldn't help feeling somewhat intimidated by the Finn's secretive yet overpowering presence. Of all the team members, the Archer was the only one he had trouble talking to; even

Blackie Sullivan was more approachable. So he could not hide his surprise when the Archer slid the file he had been looking at towards him.

"Take a look at this, will you?" Jukka said.

Ben opened the file and saw a copy of the front page of *The Globe* devoted to the attack on the city. He had, in fact, freelanced for that well-known and reputable newspaper in the past. There was an editorial discussing the role of Hexagon: were they the saviors of the city, or indirectly responsible for the assault in the first place?

"Nothing out of the ordinary," Ra said after reading the article. "Even if the team is popular, there will always be those who question whether or not we're the ones attracting this kind of misfortune by our very presence."

The Mysterious Archer smiled.

"I'm not interested in that article," he said. "Look at that little insert at the bottom of the page."

Ben looked back at the paper. There, in smaller print, near the bottom, was an item of lesser importance:

Daring burglary at the Metropolitan Museum of Art

He turned the pages to follow the story and learned that, taking advantage of the chaos in Manhattan, thieves had stolen an item from the Museum's Egyptian collection. It was called the "Eye of Udjat."

"What does that have to do with us?" asked Ben, clearly confused. "This seems rather like a trivial matter."

The Archer shrugged and kept smiling.

"Let's review," he said, counting on his fingers. "One, the Museum was within the Xans' attack perimeter. Two, the burglary took place during this attack, or at least when the police were too busy to care. Three, the object stolen is an Egyptian antique, and finally, four, your hero's name specifically refers to that country's mythology. That makes four good reasons to go and investigate this together, don't you think?"

Ra remained silent under the Finn's unreadable gaze. He had the feeling that Jukka was testing him in some mysterious fashion.

"Why not?" he said, pretending not to care. "That at least will keep us busy while we wait for Cendrine and Dominik to return. And as long as we stay in New York, we can respond to any emergency."

Satisfied, the Mysterious Archer nodded and the two heroes left Hexagon's HQ to look into what seemed, at first glance, to be an unimportant news item.

CHAPTER IV
The Gateway of the Gods

The entire area surrounding the Metropolitan Museum of Art had been fairly devastated and numerous construction engines were now busy clearing the access roads to allow some traffic to go through. Haggard residents wandered the streets, picking up the scattered debris of their former lives. The National Guard was still assisting the NYPD—which had paid a heavy price during the battle—in maintaining order.

Jukka Häyhä had chosen to wear a black suit that, with the dark sunglasses, made him look like some kind of official. Ben Leonard, on the other hand, was happy remaining casual and wore only jeans and a t-shirt. They had walked all the way from their HQ and couldn't help clenching their fists at the scale of the devastation.

When they reached the museum, they found themselves in front of a security cordon, but the Finn took a card out of his jacket and presented it to the officer in charge.

"Jukka Häyhä, Interpol," he introduced himself. "And this is Ben Leonard, archaeological consultant. We're here to ask a few questions about yesterday's robbery."

The policeman, at first astonished, glanced at the id and stared at the Archer.

"Interpol?" he asked. "How on Earth can this concern you?"

"Similar robberies have occurred at the British Museum and the Louvre. Egyptian antiquities, too. So we'd like to take a look around and see if we're not dealing with the same gang."

The police hesitated, then sighed and suddenly looked very tired.

"OK, go in and ask for Detective Trumbo; he's in charge of the investigation. He's inside right now."

"Thank you, officer."

Jukka and Ben entered the museum. The Met's Egyptian collection was world-famous. It took visitors on a fabulous journey back through time to an era when Pharaohs ruled over the Nile Delta, pyramids rose to challenge the Heavens themselves, and beast-headed gods were worshipped throughout the land. Priceless exhibits were on display, including the Temple of Dendur, rebuilt entirely stone by stone in one wing of the museum. Surrounded by a basin, it was located in a large room with a view over Central Park, providing a setting conducive to meditation.

Detective Trumbo, a young African-American with a mirthful smile, was sitting on a small bench facing the temple, lost in thought. The Archer handed him his Interpol id card and gave him the same speech that he had given to the officer on duty.

"...And if you could tell us more about the M.O. of these thieves, perhaps we could see if it matches that of the ones who robbed the Louvre and the British Museum," he concluded.

Trumbo examined the Archer from head to toe, as if to assess who he was dealing with. He then handed him a file containing a few photos.

"There you have it," he said in a tired voice. "That's all we have."

Jukka went through the file, which showed pictures of a medallion in the shape of a stylized eye drawn in the

Egyptian style. It had been finely crafted out of pure gold but did not look that valuable at first glance. The Archer passed the photographs to Ben.

"The Eye of Udjat," confirmed the young man, "also known as the Eye of Horus, supposedly a symbol of protection. It's a fairly common artifact."

Detective Trumbo got up and took a few steps. He reached for a pack of chewing gum in his pocket, but remembered where he was and put it back inside.

"Could you tell us what actually happened, Detective?" asked the Archer.

"Follow me, I'd rather you saw it with your own eyes."

The detective took Jukka and Ben to another room, one of the walls of which had been neatly torn aside, as if it had been hit by an armored truck. One could see the outside of the building through the opening. A glass display case stood in the middle of the room; it, too, had been broken. It was obvious that the stolen Eye had been inside it.

The Archer scanned the room, analyzing every detail with his characteristic meticulousness.

"This is where the robbery took place," commented Trumbo. "During the alien attack, the break in triggered the security system. All the museum entrances were immediately sealed off. Visitors and staff were trapped inside, which in a way was a good thing, because it kept them safe. The museum was not attacked by the Crocs. The guards heard a loud crash and they rushed in here—and that's when it gets complicated..."

Trumbo walked to the front of the hole in the wall and finally started chewing on a piece of gum. A smile of satisfaction lit up his face.

"All the witnesses told the same story," he continued. "It's tempting to believe that they were the victims of some kind of collective hallucination... According to the guards, they were transported to Ancient Egypt, to the banks of the Nile, under a bright sun. And when they finally came back to their senses... Well, that's what they saw..."

"Did you have time to interview all the witnesses?" Ben wondered. "What, with everything that's been happening..."

Trumbo smiled.

"The Met isn't just any kind of museum, guys. When its director says, 'jump,' my Captain says 'how high, sir?' But if it makes you feel any better, it's just been me here and the two men outside. We can't spare any manpower at the moment. So to answer your question, Mr. Leonard, no, I haven't had time to interview *all* the witnesses, but what I got was enough to get an idea of what happened here, as far-fetched as it may seem."

Meanwhile, he Archer was examining the debris of surrounding the hole in the wall, paying closer attention to some chunks of concrete.

"That's very helpful, Detective Trumbo. Thank you," he said. "Can we keep that picture of the Eye?"

"If you like. Here's my card. If you find anything more, let us know. Otherwise, if nothing turns up, we'll have no choice but move on to another case quickly."

"You can count on me."

Jukka shook the detective's hand, and the two Hexagoneers left the museum.

The Mysterious Archer and Ra were now eating hot dogs, sitting on a bench in Central Park like two ordinary New Yorkers. Life was slowly returning to the Big Apple with its cortege of joggers and street peddlers.

Jukka, perfectly relaxed, enjoyed his hot dog while relaxing in the beautiful sun-drenched afternoon. Ben, on the other hand, seemed upset.

"You could have told me that these other museums had also been robbed," he complained.

"As far as I know, they haven't," replied the Archer. "I made it up to gain entrance at the Met. It seemed like a good idea."

Ben almost choked on his wiener.

"But what if they had checked? Did you think about that? And where does that Interpol card come from?"

"Ah. That's something of a long story. Our Brotherhood has an, er, unadvertised connection with Interpol. You scratch my back, I scratch yours sort of thing. So the card is authentic. As for my little lie, I didn't think that our brave police officers would have the time or the inclination to check it out. Besides, after what happened yesterday, I don't think the NYPD will have much time to devote to that robbery, no matter what Detective Trumbo told us."

Ben didn't know what to say. The aplomb of the Archer had left him speechless. The Finn finished his hot dog, then crumpled the greasy wrapper into a ball and threw it into a garbage can ten feet away from their bench. Despite the distance and the light breeze, the crumpled ball of paper landed exactly where it was supposed to.

"Let's review," the Finn continued. "This robbery is clearly the work of superhumans. The wall wasn't smashed by a truck or a battering ram, but by someone using his bare hands. The fist marks on some of the concrete debris speak for themselves. As for the collective

Egyptian hallucination the guards experienced, it must have been caused by an individual with psychic powers."

Once again, Ra felt scrutinized by his teammate who had looked at him sharply as he finished his sentence.

"Raw physical power and mind control. These are powers that rarely go together. So we can deduce that there are at least two suspects," concluded the Archer.

Ben, having nothing to contribute so far, decided to take another look at the photo that Detective Trumbo had let them borrow. Now that he was looking at it closely, the reporter felt a certain familiarity with the object. A few details, the interlacing of two strokes, the bent of a curve, seemed to awaken dormant memories...

"Does this Eye speak to you?" asked the Mysterious Archer, ever vigilant.

"I don't know... At first glance, it looks like an ordinary Eye of Udjat, but I think that there's something more about it... I can't quite put my finger on it."

Jukka leaned forward towards Ben.

"So now that we know that this theft was committed by unidentified but powerful superhumans, do you still think this case is a 'trivial matter,' as you put it earlier?"

"No, I'll admit you were right. This definitely deserves to be looked into," Ben replied with a hint of annoyance. "But we have no more clues about the perpetrators than Detective Trumbo."

The Archer stood up and stretched his legs, offering his pale face framed by light blond hair to the heat of the sun.

"That's what you think. I happen to have a couple of art specialists among my contacts. Why don't we pay them a visit?"

Jill Temple and John Harper were a particularly charming couple with impeccable manners. She was a beautiful blonde with refined elegance; he had the distinguished appearance of an English lord. At first glance, their air of complicity was obvious—they were in their early thirties, yet they seemed to have had many adventures together, forging an understanding based on love and mutual respect.

They had greeted Jukka with a loud greeting, begging him to come in their plush Manhattan apartment. Ben was also greeted warmly when his companion introduced him, and the four of them found themselves in the blink of an eye in a comfortable living room, chatting around a beautiful mahogany table with a good glass of Chardonnay at hand.

Ben listened to Jill, John and Jukka chatting about various things, checking up on old friends, reminiscing about common capers... The Finn seemed perfectly at ease in this luxury apartment, socializing with this obviously very wealthy couple. The Mysterious Archer was indeed aptly named, thought Ben. The man was an enigma.

As for him, he felt out of place in his slightly ragged clothes, contrasting embarrassingly the opulent decor. While sipping his wine, Ben glanced at the many works by old masters—Escher, Van Gogh, Miro— hanging on the walls. Jill and John were indeed connoisseurs.

"So Jukka, what *really* brought you here? I guess this isn't just a social call," asked John.

The Archer took out the picture of the Eye of Udjat and put it on the table without saying a word. John took it and looked at it with a magnifying glass. Jill leaned over his shoulder, frowning. She stood up and rummaged through a bookcase before pulling out the volume she'd been looking for.

"Ah-ha! Found it!" she exclaimed with a triumphant smile.

She opened the book on a selected page and showed it to Jukka and John. Ben joined them and saw a picture showing an Eye remarkably similar to the one that had been stolen. The Archer spent a long minute comparing the two images before rendering his verdict.

"It's definitely the same. You haven't lost your eye, Jill."

"In this case, it was easy. This Eye was part of a set that John and I, er, were very interested in at one time," she replied, blushing slightly.

Jukka nodded with a knowing look.

"A set?" asked Ben.

John turned the pages and showed them two more pieces.

"Here's an Ankh and a Hekka scepter. It's like a jigsaw puzzle. If you put the Eye and these other two relics together, you get an object called the Gateway of the Gods. In Ancient Egypt, it was supposed to open a passage between the world of men and that of the gods. The priests claimed to use it to hear the will of Ra or Osiris."

Ben again felt that these images and the words were awakening long buried memories, still distant and vague, but very real.

The Gateway of the Gods...

He knew that this was somehow connected to his secret origins. Tearing himself away from his thoughts, he suddenly realized that he had become the center of attention—especially from the Archer, who was staring at him, frowning.

"Ben, you're like an archaeologist. Does this mean something to you? Jukka asked.

"Maybe," Ben replied, embarrassed. "If our thieves are looking for this Gateway of the Gods, they'll need the other two artifacts to complete it." He added to divert attention away.

Jill and John reacted with amazement.

"The Eye of Udjat Eye has been stolen?" asked the beautiful blonde. "But wasn't it on display at the Met?"

"Yes, it was," confirmed Jukka. "But thieves stole it last week during all the chaos caused by the alien attack."

"Ah!" exclaimed John, suddenly struck by a thought. "Two days ago, the Egyptian Museum at Turin was also robbed. I barely paid any attention to it at the time, but now…"

He opened his laptop and ran a quick search.

"There! There's even is photo of what was stolen: a solid gold Ankh adorned with jewels. It seems as if the thieves didn't take anything else. The article is by one Leonardo Verga. He says that the Italian police believes that the perps used some type of hallucinogenic gas to commit their crime without being seen. The guards were plunged into a hypnotic trance…"

Jukka elbowed Ben's side.

"You see, I wasn't that far off with my story about the Louvre and the British Museum. Not that I'm happy about it."

"This means that the thieves now only need one relic to open the Gateway of the Gods," said Ben. "All we need to know is where the Hekka Scepter is and we can catch them, assuming they haven't already taken it."

"I don't think they have," said John, searching n his laptop. "It's being kept at the Boston Museum of Fine Arts and they're not reporting any burglaries."

Jukka got up, dragging Ben with him.

"Excellent!" he said. "Jill, John, thank you. As always, your expertise was invaluable."

"No need for thanks, my friend," replied John. "We owe much to the Brotherhood of Archers, and if we can be of service in return..."

"I don't suppose you're going to tell us anything more about this case?" Jill asked with a smile on her face.

"After we solve it, I promise you you'll be the first to know," said the Archer.

Then he turned towards his partner.

"What say you to a ride to Boston, Ben?"

The journalist nodded pensively. This story had touched him more closely than he had thought; he was now curious to discover the identity of the thieves who had stolen these relics which evoked such familiar echoes in his mind.

CHAPTER V
The Abandoned Base

Black Lys, the Dark Flyer and Sweet flew over the Amazon in one of the many specialized, retrofitted and souped up jets that NeroTek kept at Hexagon's disposal—the Hexajet having been brought in for much needed repairs. Dominik was as usual at the controls, maneuvering the aircraft according to his girlfriend's instructions. The spiky-haired young prodigy had her eyes glued to a monitor with lines of code and satellite maps of the area. She was trying to pinpoint the precise location of the secret base she had located nearby. The jungle below was so dense that the plane could easily fly over its location a dozen times without them noticing it.

Cendrine was sitting in a comfortable armchair, behind the cockpit. She looked out through a window, her eyes lost in thoughts. The Xans, Melanos... All this brought back old memories, of a time when the world seemed so much simpler. She had been so very young when Hexagon had been founded, barely twenty, but she remembered that time vividly. The original team had gathered around an alien from Zhud named Aster and his Earth girlfriend Pinky to defeat the sinister schemes of Aster's arch-enemy, the tyrant Melanos. After an epic battle, and their ultimate triumph, the six heroes—seven, counting Pinky, but that was a different, less enlightened time!—had decided to remain united and band together to continue defending the world against major threats.

She had also be there when White Mask had quit Hexagon in anger after the disastrous affair of the Black

Hive, Aster (whose genetic code was so close to that of humans) had mysteriously vanished on his way back to Zhud, and Jeff Sullivan (who had quickly became their first leader) had died on the Moon at the hands of their arch-foe the Necromancer... She had been there when the first Dark Flyer (Dominik's father) had wisely decided to retire, and Dax, the original Mysterious Archer, with whom she had shared a liaison, had suddenly been summoned back by the Brotherhood... She remembered romancing the powerful Gun Gallon, then exiled from his adopted homeworld of Orios, before he had had to return there to fight Togor Tog...

Cendrine de Mérignan was feeling depressed when she thought about it all. Of course, the lives of superheroes were dangerous and everyone on the team was aware of this, but that didn't stop the mourning and the grief when one of them fell in battle or disappeared without explanation like Aster had. Deep down inside, the Black Lys was hoping to find a clue, a lead, anything that would allow her to find Aster, their missing teammate without whom Hexagon would not exist.

"Cendrine, you're being very quiet back there?" Dominik remarked.

"Yes, I was, wasn't I? I'm sorry... I was lost in my thoughts. Thinking of Melanos brought back memories of Aster, and I was hoping that... that..."

"Say no more, I get it. All that happened before I joined, but Dad told me all about it. I, too, hope we can solve the mystery of his disappearance one day."

"I won't be solved on Earth, I think; we should go to Zhud."

"I've always had trouble with this concept of a negative universe," Sweet interjected, still tapping on her keyboard. "What's it like? Like some kind of parallel dimension?"

Dominik smiled. At last, something that his girl-friend didn't already know...

"Conceptually, it's easy to grasp," he said. "A negative universe is the opposite of ours. They do not occupy the same physical space, however. But they're not an alternative dimension either."

Sweet frowned. The young woman was definitely more comfortable with computers than theoretical physics.

"But to travel from our positive universe to Zhud, how do you go about it then?" she asked.

"There, the method is the same as traveling to other dimensions: you have to cross a quantum barrier in order to harmonize the vibratory structure with that of your destination. It requires precise calculations and that's why we..."

"Yes, I've got it now, please stop!" Sweet exclaimed.

What Ben had said during their meeting now made sense to her. If the Xans appeared so suddenly above New York, it was because they had materialized from another dimension, or possibly from the negative universe.

"That's right," said Cendrine, who had joined them. "Aster and Melanos controlled that tech; we never had full access to it. There are others on Earth who can dimension hop, but they use what we'd call 'magic.'"

"We might learn more if we ever locate that damn base. Where are we on that, Sweet" asked Dominik.

"I think I've got it," replied the computer scientist, holding out her finger. "What we're looking for is precisely there: in that big rocky mass."

The radar, which Sweet had linked to her computer, pointed to a location that looked like an ancient ziggurat buried under wild vegetation, barely discernible in this green hellscape.

Without a word, Dominik started the descent.

The plane was able to land in a clearing on the bank of a wide river. It took all of the Dark Flyer's skills to land accurately on such a small area.

Black Lys had donned a more comfortable version of her blue and black outfit for the occasion, to be more at ease in her movements in the stifling atmosphere of the rain forest. Dominik donned his armor, a massive battle suit of his own design with a stylized red eagle on his torso, the emblem of the Neros, just as the lily was that of the Mérignans. As for Sweet, she wore her usual and unlikely ensemble of half-torn leather and high-tech accessories, enhancing her slender silhouette and giving her access to all the gadgets she might need.

The two heroes and the young genius set off through the jungle, with the Dark Flyer leading the way, clearing a path for his companions. It took them about twenty minutes to reach the foot of the strange pyramid that Sweet had identified as a potentially active lair of the evil Melanos. The building itself looked like a pre-Columbian pyramid, except that these weren't supposed to exist in the Amazon... Plants and vines covered the stone steps and had even cracked some of them. The place looked as if it had been abandoned for years.

As they walked around, they located the entrance: a square-shaped hole cut right into the stone, that had once been closed by two heavy steel doors. But now, these had been torn off their hinges; the metal showed traces of violent blows. Dominik whistled as he calculated the power it had taken to break the doors down. He turned on his spotlight and swept the corridor just beyond the entrance. Black Lys crouched down and examined the demolished doors. She ran her fingers over the dents, identifying the recognizable shape of a fist. The conclusion was obvious: that base had been visited before by a person of superhuman strength.

"Dominik, do you detect a presence inside?" she inquired.

"Only some residual electronic activity," replied the Dark Flyer. "No signs of life except for us and some of the local wildlife."

"Good! I'd prefer to avoid a bad surprise."

Sweet was busy analyzing an entry code box located just before the door, to the right side, a complex device that had once controlled the access to the base.

"Our predecessor wasn't very patient," she finally said. "It would have taken me just under two minutes to open that door properly."

She shrugged and pulled out a flashlight before stepping inside the building, but Dominik stopped her with a gesture.

"Let me go first," he said. "Maybe there are still traps around. Melanos was a devious one..."

Black Lys manifested her bio-electric swords out of her hands, casting a bluish light on the walls of the stone corridor into which they advanced.

The exploration of the tunnels was conducted cautiously. The inside of the pyramid consisted in a mixture of stone and metal, with electronic circuitry running through the walls like veins and arteries. The Dark Flyer confirmed that it was a typical design from Zhud.

Some tunnels led to cells, laboratories, armory, living quarters... Most of the rooms were deserted, covered by a veil of dust. The building's generators ran erratically; the lights flickered with an ominous hum. The cool temperature made Cendrine shiver, but she had to admit to herself that the cold was not the only reason why she did. Everything smelled of death and desolation. Her hopes of finding Aster disappeared as she plunged into the bowels of Melanos' lair.

At various strategic points, traps appeared to have been triggered: laser cannons springing up from the ground, fire throwers meant to burn anyone who passed between them, deadly gas sprays... But all had been crushed in the same way as the entrance gate: through sheer brute force. Whoever had passed here before had not let anything slowed his progress.

Sweet suggested that they should follow the footsteps of the previous, as yet unidentified, visitor, who obviously knew where he was going. As a result, the three Hexagoneers eventually ended up in a control room, the nerve center from which Melanos had directed all his evil schemes.

Suddenly, a movement caught their attention; Black Lys and the Dark Flyer moved as one, ready for battle. But it was only robot carcasses dragging themselves pitifully on the ground, humanoid shells now reduced to a collection of scattered parts. The machines crawled towards the heroes, a flashing red glow still animating their cybernetic eyes. Designed to defend this place, the androids had been dismantled, and only a remnant of energy kept them going.

They were only soulless robots, but Cendrine couldn't help but feel some pity for them when she saw them wriggling so miserably. In a gesture of compassion, she used her blades to put a definitive end to their misery. Without further ado, Sweet headed for the main console which had been gutted and emptied of some of its components. She took out various electronic gadgets from her many pockets and plugged them in.

"What are you looking for?" asked the Dark Flyer.

"I'm trying to access the main server," she replied without stopping her activities. "To find out what was stolen. Damn it! The language must be that of Zhud! I'm going to have to download my translation software from HQ, but the satellite reception is terrible..."

Sweet punched the computer, whose screen blinked on for a moment. The young woman grumbled and set about writing a complex decryption program. Dominik thought it would be safer to get away from her.

"It's not what you expected," he said to Black Lys.

"It sure isn't," she replied with a sigh. "I had hoped... I don't know... That we would find something useful."

Dominik understood that she was referring to the mystery of Aster's disappearance and placed his imposing metal hand gently on her shoulder.

"We still might, you never know. Sweet works miracles. She may find answers."

Cendrine smiled at him, but her gaze remained fixed far away.

"Bingo!" Sweet suddenly exclaimed. "I've got to the mainframe. I'm accessing the database. So... It looks like we're in a transdimensional center. From what I'm seeing, this was where the calculations required to cross dimensions were performed. And it is the hard drive containing the navigation protocols that was stolen by our mysterious intruder, along with two negative fusion reactors... which I know nothing about."

"Energy sources powerful enough to open a passage between dimensions," answered the Dark Flyer, thoughtful. "It now appears likely that those who broke into this base did it in order to steal this technology, and if so, they might be the ones behind the Xans' attack."

"Right!" said Cendrine. "Then Melanos can't be the one behind it, because he wouldn't need to steal from himself. So we are dealing with an unknown enemy, who has plans to travel between dimensions and strike at Earth—which he can now do without warning, wherever he wants."

All three thought about the implications of this discovery. The recollection of Manhattan devastated by Xan fire, the death and the destruction, gave pause for thought.

"Let's return to HQ," Cendrine decided. "We need to inform the rest of the team."

CHAPTER VI
A Bad Night at the Museum

It was already dark when Ra and the Mysterious Archer arrived in Boston. They had first stopped by Hexagon's HQ in order to pick up some supplies and tell Rakar and Blackie Sullivan where they were going, and why. The master of dark matter had just shrugged before returning to his exercise. The shaman, on the other hand, duties, had been very interested by the story of the Gateway of the Gods. He promised his teammates to do some research on his own and talk to some of his contacts in the magical community.

The journey between New York and Boston took three, long, seemingly interminable hours. The Archer was driving and made very little conversation. Ben Leonard knew that Jukka was something of an anomaly within Hexagon, because he owed his primary allegiance to the Brotherhood of Archers of Graxonia, and was only "on loan"—if one could call it that!—to the Group. Jukka was a lone wolf, with his own network of informants, as Ben had just realized. He was sure that the Archer knew a great deal more about him than he had let out, and that he hadn't brought him with him by accident.

Ben wanted very much to find out what the Archer knew about his strange past, but at the same time, he was also a little afraid of finding out. So he was greatly relieved when they arrived at last in Boston.

Now the two heroes were waiting inconspicuously on a small deserted square overlooking Huntington Avenue, not far from the Museum of Fine Arts.

The Archer had taken a pair of binoculars out of his uniform and was scanning the place carefully despite the darkness. Ra sat on a bench next to him and reflected on the latest series of events.

"It doesn't make any sense!" he suddenly exclaimed. "If the attack on New York was a mere diversion to allow our thieves to enter the Met and steal the Eye, it's like swatting flies with a bazooka!"

The Archer shrugged but did not stop scanning their target.

"I've seen stranger things," he replied. "At this stage in our investigation, I'm not ruling out anything. It may only be a coincidence, but I find it troubling. An alien attack occurs just as an Egyptian antiquity is stolen by superhumans... Plus the fact that it may be connected to you..."

Ra was uncomfortable that his teammate had mentioned this at all, but at least he had done it in a non-accusatory manner.

"I agree," he sighed. "There may be a connection. But note that in Turin, the local museum was robbed without any kind of diversion. If Boston is to be attacked by more Xans, there isn't much that you and I will be able to do... It still seems like a stretch to me..."

"You must learn to be patient, Ben. This isn't like a fight with other superhumans when you think mostly with your fists. Right now, we're gathering clues and trying to solve a puzzle. We don't have enough elements to reach a fully formed conclusion, one way or another. And if the Xans do return, we'll alert the others."

Ben Leonard got up from the bench and started pacing.

"Who is to say that the thieves will strike tonight?" he asked.

"They have only one item left to retrieve in order to complete the Gateway of the Gods," replied the Mysterious Archer. "If I were them, I would strike now, while the iron is hot, as the saying goes. Worst case, we'll spend a few nights out keeping watch. But I know a good hotel in the neighborhood, if you'd like to take a break?"

Ra was about to rebuff the offer when he suddenly stiffened. He felt a sensation that he had not experienced for a long time. He used his ESP to probe the Museum. The Archer had noticed his reaction and lowered his binoculars.

"What have you detected?" he inquired.

"They're here," Ra answered.

Ra opened his shirt, revealing his golden uniform and the black sun emblazoned on it. Then, surrounded by his glowing aura, he rose into the air.

"I'll go ahead and draw them out," he said. "Then you can take them by surprise."

The Archer nodded and quickly assembled his bow as his teammate flew towards the museum.

Ra forced the doors of the building open by telekinesis. He levitated through its dark, empty corridors until he saw a few security guards and two cleaning women. They stood motionless, staring blankly at a wall, caught in some kind of trance. The hero approached one of the guards and made telepathic contact with his mind. He was plunged immediately into a maelstrom of illusions, false images imposed on the man's psyche to keep him in a state of impotence. This web of hallucinations was like a barrier that prevented him from reaching the guard's mind. His own psionic powers were thwarted by the illusions created by his unknown foe.

With a sigh, Ra broke contact. His telepathic powers were considerable, but not on the same level as those of a Master Telepath from the Galactic Federation like Jaleb. His main advantage lay with telekinesis. In the realm of the mind, he was no match for the one who had created these hallucinations, and whose identity he now was beginning to suspect. He had to take the fight onto a more physical arena if he wished to have a chance to win. Deploying his golden aura, he quickly set off towards the Egyptian wing.

With a simple mental command, Ra broke down the doors of the vast room containing the rarest pieces from the Egyptology department. As he expected, the thieves were already there, looking for the Hekka scepter, the last missing piece to complete the Gateway of the Gods. There was an elderly man with a long white beard braided into a point, dressed in a toga, his head topped with a tall headdress decorated with a black scarab. He opened his eyes wide when he saw Ben arrive with a loud crash.

Next to him stood a woman of unusual beauty, whose green eyes with slit pupils contrasted with her matt skin and hair so black that it absorbed the light. She, too, was wearing a toga, whose folds highlighted her voluptuous body. She glanced at Ra with an amused expression as he landed in front of her companion.

Ben addressed the two intruders.

"Athor... I thought I sensed your presence here... I was not mistaken."

"Prince Ra, it is a pleasure to see you again after all these years," replied the older man with a touch of irony, making a slight curtsy.

"If you're here, I imagine that my accursed brother is not far," said Ben. "Tell me, where the hell is Set hiding?"

"Patience my prince, you'll find out soon enough."

With an expression of contempt, Ben turned to the young woman.

"What about you, Bastet? I can't believe you're siding with him."

"My handsome prince, the life of an Immortal is so long and Heliopolis is such a dull place," she said softly. "Set promised me distractions beyond my imagination, and I see that he was telling the truth," she added, putting a caressing hand on Ra's chest.

The hero grabbed her wrist with an iron fist, his eyes angry.

"That's enough!" he thundered. "I don't know what you're up to, or what my brother's plans are, but you're going to come with me and answer all my questions."

Bastet hissed like an angry cat and, with a supple gesture, released himself from Ra's grip. With superhuman speed, she slapped him on the face. The hero took a step back, his cheek cut by the young woman's fingernails which had grown several inches and become sharp claws.

"Damn it!" he murmured.

Ra gathered all his psychic power preparing for a fight; the floor and the walls of the room began to shake.

"Amon!" shouted Athor. "Come to us!"

The wall facing the outside of the museum exploded, throwing debris and dust all around. A third person rushed through the opening and towards Ra. The hero had barely enough time to set up a telekinetic screen before the newcomer hit him with tremendous force. Ben felt his psychic shield weaken under the sheer power of the blow. His concentration broke and he was thrown backwards, crashing into a display case.

The hero got back to his feet painfully, the attack having shaken him badly. He took time to study this new and unexpected opponent whom Athor had named Amon. He was a medium-sized man, solidly built. Unlike his two companions, he was not wearing a toga but a dark green uniform with the black scarab symbol on his chest—the emblem of Set. But most intriguing was the golden mask with neutral features that covered his entire face, making it impossible to identify him or read his expressions. The newcomer clenched his fists, ready to attack again.

Ra tried to reach his mind and had another surprise, for he found nothing in it. Amon was only an empty shell, a living puppet animated by an inflexible will. He recognized the mental signature of his brother Set, whose telepathic control had probably crushed Amon's soul—if he ever had one. At the very edge of his consciousness, Ben sensed the various hallucinations projected by Athor, likely the greatest illusion-caster in the world. He concentrated all his telepathic abilities to protect himself from them.

Ra decided to attack despite the pain hammering his skull. Wrapping himself with his mental shield, he took off and hit Amon, delivering a powerful punch amplified by his telekinetic power—but in vain. The man with the golden mask didn't even stagger. Instead, he grabbed Ra's wrist and twisted it before throwing the young hero violently against a wall. Ben barely had time to slow down before hitting the concrete surface; he screamed in pain from the shock. Without giving him time to breathe, Amon rose into the air and fell back on him, feet forward. The shield that Ben tried to raise to protect himself shattered and he found himself embedded in the ground, spitting blood, with several broken ribs broke.

He only managed to get up thanks to a truly superhuman effort and blasted his foe with a telekinetic bolt that pushed Amon back to the other side of the room.

Athor watched the fight gloating while Bastet seized the Hekka scepter. Ben's vision was blurry. As far as he could remember, he'd never been beaten so badly. He held his sides, short of breath. He felt the metallic taste of blood on his tongue. Gathering his last ounce of strength, he levitated the most massive objects in the room and threw them at Amon. A shower of stones fell upon the strange warrior in the golden mask, who soon found himself buried under a makeshift pyramid. Ra turned towards Athor and Bastet.

"Put down that scepter and surrender," he ordered, trying to not let his pain show. "This is my last warning."

"Arrogant fool!" spat Athor. "Amon is not so easily dispatched."

Bastet burst out laughing as the stone prison created by Ra exploded. Amon emerged from under the debris without a scratch, just some dust on his clothes. He showed no signs of fatigue or shortness of breath.

Ra felt his heart pounding. He projected wave after wave of psychic energy against his foe but managed only to slow him down as Amon moved inexorably towards him like an unstoppable force. Pushed against a corner, Ben saw a murderous fist rise and understood that he was going to die, perhaps for the second time in his long existence.

The Mysterious Archer had decided not to follow his teammate in order to try to take their enemies by surprise. As a soldier, he knew the value of a good surprise attack and he had made this his specialty for a long time. He knew that he was less powerful than most of the other Hexagoneers, but he had undergone training that few of them could understand, except perhaps Rakar who was a former Marine. The Archer always tried to be prepared for any eventuality, even when facing an unknown adversary, and his natural gift to foresee everything in an almost manic way had only increased since he had fought the Five Venoms a few months ago. Tortured to almost the point of death, he had had to reveal the security codes of their HQ and he still hadn't forgiven himself. Under his tongue, he felt the hollow tooth in which he had hidden a cyanide capsule to prevent a reoccurrence of that scenario. He would rather die than fail his teammates again.

Knowing that they were about to tackle some superhuman foes, he had taken great care to equip himself accordingly. His orange-and-crimson uniform was reinforced with kevlar and hexagonium plates—a gift from the Dark Flyer—to protect himself as thoroughly as possible. In his balaclava, he had concealed a neuro-scrambler in order to thwart any psychic attack. His weaponry remained the same: a heavy crossbow capable of firing high velocity shots at amazing speed and a whole arsenal of projectiles hidden all over him. His usual tonfas were kept in a holster attached to his thighs. With this, he believed he could win a fight against any mid-level superhuman, or at least foster that illusion long enough to work out a Plan B if the opposition was more powerful than he had expected.

When his telepathic contact with Ra was suddenly cut off, the Mysterious Archer realized at once that things had gotten serious. He hastened to rejoin his teammate, circling the building. Then he heard a loud crash, like an exploding stone wall, and remembered the scene at the Met. When he finally reached the location, he saw that the wall of the museum had been breached. He leapt inside and swept the room, using his formidable sense of tactical analysis. First, he saw a beautiful young woman holding the Hekka scepter with an old man by her side, his back turned to him. Finally, he saw a badly wounded Ra, cornered against a wall, facing a masked opponent preparing to deliver a death blow.

No sooner had the scene been imprinted in his mind than the Mysterious Archer sprang into action. He fired first at the man in the golden mask, then at the beautiful woman.

The first arrow hit Amon in the chest and exploded, releasing ten thousand volts. The titan felt the blow and was forced to retreat, his body shaking.

The second arrow, the tip of which unfolded as a half-moon hook, ripped the scepter out of Bastet's hands and nailed it to a wall.

Now that their three foes were alerted to his presence, the Archer also set off a beacon, summoning the rest of Hexagon.

"Ben, are you all right?" he asked telepathically.

"Not really. I can't protect you from the illusions of Athor—that's the old man. I have to save my strength for my telekinesis."

"I'll neutralize him next, then."

The Mysterious Archer felt a mental prong attempt to pierce the defenses of his mind; his neuro-scrambler was almost overwhelmed by the vast psychic power that assailed him. Jukka blinked and found himself suddenly thrown into a desert with warriors armed with curved swords surrounding him. He immediately realized that this was but an illusion, but one so real that he could feel the burning sun on his skin, hear the cries of the men around him, breathe the sand lifted by the wind...

This false reality was fearsome, capable of trapping even the most sophisticated of heroes. But the Archer didn't succumb to it. He knew that he was still in the Boston Museum of Fine Arts. He had memorized the lay out of the place before entering it; so he fired his cross-bow without the least hesitation in the direction he knew was the correct one. Suddenly, a scream pierced the veil of illusion which then tore in front of his eyes.

Now he could see Athor on his knees not too far away—his shoulder pierced by his bolt. The old man's face showed deep hatred. The Archer was about to finish him off, when a figure leapt at him with astonishing agil-ity. He raised his weapon just in time to block the sharp claws aimed at his eyes. Bastet hissed aggressively as they engaged in close combat. The woman was moving at superhuman speed, making a series of feints and at-tacks without giving her opponent time to breathe. Only the Mysterious Archer's gift of anticipating his enemy's moves enabled him to dodge her potentially deadly blows.

Ra felt his fears recede now that Amon appeared to have been neutralized. He caught his breath and threw a telekinetic bolt at Bastet to throw her off balance. She screamed as she stumbled, and the Archer took ad-vantage of that to punch her solidly in the face. But the green-eyed woman got up with a murderous gleam in her eyes. Meanwhile, Amon succeeded in finally over-coming the effects of the electric shocks and crushed the arrow that had been delivering them between his powerful fingers. Athor, still holding his wounded shoulder, grabbed the Hekka scepter, tearing it away from the wall before slipping it under his toga.

The Mysterious Archer pulled a slender dart out of his uniform and fired it at Ra. The dart went into his thigh and the hero suddenly felt a surge of new energy running through his body.

"A small pick-me-up of my composition," explained Jukka. *"Adrenalin and amphetamines. Temporary effect only, sadly."*

"That'll do for now. Thanks!"

Ra concentrated all his mental power and focused it on Amon. He encircled his muscular body with telekinetic rings intended to immobilize him, or at least slow him down. Meanwhile, the Archer understood that Bastet was far from being an ordinary foe: her claws had torn his kevlar suit like silk. He fired three arrows into the ceiling. They began to emit a thick smoke that quickly filled the entire room. Then, having memorized his enemies' positions, he fired another round of explosive arrows at them. The three adversaries began to retreat towards the exit.

"Let us withdraw, we have what we came for," said the voice of Athor.

"The mortal will pay for this," uttered Bastet. "We will meet again..."

Ra threw all his psychic force on the ceiling and caused a section of it to collapse in order to stop their enemies, but in vain. They heard a brief buzzing sound and then silence returned.

The Boston P.D. showed up shortly thereafter. None of the museum employees had any recollection of what had happened. They all told the same story, describing the Egyptian illusions that had kept them away from the crime scene. Ra and the Mysterious Archer, however, were able to give the officers a full report on what had really happened. Their status as Hexagoneers gave weight to their testimony and they were soon free to go.

However, the Archer chose to lurk around the museum for a little longer. He crouched in the very spot where Athor, Bastet and Amon must have stood before they disappeared. Their footsteps on the grass were clear, but disappeared abruptly as if they had simply vanished. Which, of course, was the case, according to Ra. The young man theorized that had used teleportation in order to escape.

They were well aware that they had suffered a defeat. Their enemies had seized the scepter, and, if the battle had dragged on, they would likely have been defeated too because of Amon's raw power. Ben was seriously wounded; his face was swollen, his sides hurt because of his broken ribs, which also impacted his breathing. Now that the effects of the drug cocktail that the Archer had injected in him was wearing off, he could barely stand. However, he had politely rejected the offer of an ambulance to take him to Boston General.

The Mysterious Archer decided to take advantage of his teammate's weakness to find some answers.

"All right, Ben," he said in a deceptively friendly voice. "We've just faced three superhumans with names, looks and powers reminiscent of Ancient Egypt, just like you, and who fled using a teleportation device that may well be the same that brought the Xans to New York. Don't you think it's time you told us what this is all about?"

Ra avoided his gaze but sat, or rather collapsed, next to him. Confronted to his stubborn silence, Jukka persisted.

"Look, I had you investigated when you joined Hexagon. I know you're not exactly what you pretend to be, even though even the Brotherhood wasn't able to discover your true origins..."

"OK, you're right!" Ben finally said. "I've been keeping things away from you and I'm sorry about it. I wasn't trying to be deceptive or something like that. I just felt it was my personal business and no one else's. But I realize now that I should tell you everything in light of what just happened..."

"Good. But keep it for the entire team. I think they're here. I can hear the Hexajet."

Ra heard a muted whooshing sound and looked up. He recognized the silhouette of the plane in the night sky. He suddenly felt really old—as old as he really was...

CHAPTER VII
The Immortals

After the distress call sent by the Mysterious Archer, Rakar and Blackie Sullivan had rushed aboard the now-repaired Hexajet, but had been too late to join the confrontation.

Back at their New York HQ, Ra enjoyed a couple of hours of rest in the infirmary where the best medibots NeroTek had ever created attended his wounds. The healing drones worked ceaselessly around him, injecting him with nanomachines, repairing his body and bombarding him with vita-rays. During that time, he kept thinking about what he was going tell the other Hexagoneers and the way he would present the truth to them.

Ben realized that, now, he had to tell them the full truth about him, so that they could get better prepared to fight the enemies that had been exposed and that he knew so well. He knew that a full confession would be a somewhat difficult thing to do, but he had to give the rest of the team a good idea of the threat that lay ahead. What he feared above all was the possible loss of the trust from his comrades, a trust that he had worked so hard to earn during the last few weeks. And now more than ever—if his hunch proved to be correct—he would need the world's most powerful heroes at his side...

While Ben Leonard mulled over these thoughts, Black Lys, the Dark Flyer and Sweet had returned from South America and briefed their teammates about what they had discovered in Melanos' abandoned base. In turn, the Mysterious Archer had told them about what had happened in Boston. A meeting had been called for the next day. Then Jukka had gone to see Ra in the infirmary to tell him to be ready to talk.

There was a heavy silence in the meeting room at Hexagon's HQ. Ben Leonard could feel the eyes of all his teammates converging on him. The doubts he saw on their faces were more painful than the wounds he had received the night before.

The meeting began with a detailed report from Cendrine about their exploration of Melanos' lair. Holographic pictures enabled everyone to visualize what was being reported by the Black Lys: the doors broken down by superhuman force, the booby traps neutralized, the robots dismantled... But above all, the hardware stolen from the control room by the mysterious intruders, including devices designed for making safe transdimensional trips and negative fusion reactors.

This only increased Ra's concerns. The hero didn't like the picture that was slowly forming in his mind.

"So we found both answers and questions," concluded Black Lys. "There is no doubt in my mind that the looting of Melanos' base is related to the attack on New York."

Ben felt the gaze of the Mysterious Archer. He had a lump in his throat and a dry mouth.

"Rakar, Blackie, is there anything new to report on your end?" asked Cendrine.

"Nothing at all," replied the shaman. "Ordinary crimes have even gone down since the attack."

"So let's move on to Jukka. You called this meeting, Archer. We're listening."

The Mysterious Archer began by recounting the previous day's events, starting with their visit to the Met, their conversation with detective Trumbo, their meeting with Jill and John, and their subsequent trip to Boston. He emphasized how what had seemed at first glance an opportunistic burglary had turned out to be much more, and mentioned the Gateway of the Gods. When he told his teammates about their fight against their three superpowered foes, everyone was hanging to his every word. The Finn's report was precise and detailed, especially with respect to their enemies' powers.

"I searched various databases," he concluded. "Athor, Bastet and Amon are not on file anywhere. Not in C.L.A.S.H.'s Diamond Files, not at Bureau X, not even in our archives at the Brotherhood of Archers. They appear to have sprung out of nowhere, not unlike our friend Ra..."

Ben saw his teammates' gaze turn to him. They knew how to draw their own conclusions.

"Ben, I think the time has come to shed some light on all of this," the Finn encouraged him, in a surprisingly friendly tone.

Black Lys also gave him an understanding smile which made the young man feel better. He took a long breath and launched himself into a story that he had kept to himself for far too long.

"All right," he began. "First, I want to apologize to you. I did indeed keep some things about my past secret from you. It wasn't meant to be malicious, but... let's just say that I have a rather complicated past, and I didn't want to muddle our relationship. I joined Hexagon because I needed—need—some powerful allies in anticipation of a battle that I know now is inevitable. I didn't try using you; I merely wanted you to be at my side when some of the terrible events that I foresee will occur..."

Using the keyboard in front of him, he brought up the holo-photographs that the lenses on the Mysterious Archer's headgear had taken of Athor, Bastet and Amon.

"I've known Athor and Bastet for, er, a long time. They belong to the same race as I. They work for my evil brother, Set, who wants me dead and seeks to rule the world..."

"Whoa, slow down a little here!" Dominik Nero interrupted. "What do you mean, 'same race'? According to our files, your father is American and your mother French—both deceased. And they look no more like Egyptians than I a grizzly bear. Who is this 'Set' character and what are you talking about?"

Ben sighed. He knew it wasn't going to be easy.

"I'm going to tell you everything from the beginning—which goes back a long way—but you must be patient. It might take a while. Millions of years ago, in the era that we, today, call Pangea, there lived on Earth a race some call the First Humanity. They were men and women of great stature, legendary figures such as Prince Kabur. It was a time of cosmic battles because the First Humanity wasn't alone on the planet. There were the powerful Danaians, who had preceded Mankind, and the mighty Fomores, who came from dying Mars, and later came the vampiric Wan Lords from beyond the stars, and the inhabitants of Mu, the fifth planet..."

"I think we know of the Fomores already," interjected Cendrine. "We fought one of them not long ago—Ghool."

"True. But let me continue. There is much more o come. A day came when the Muvian settlers on Earth demanded their independence and, in the ensuing conflict, Mu was destroyed, leaving behind what we know today as the asteroid belt. Earth was equally devastated.

Its continents broke up, its oceans dried up and many species became extinct, such as the fabled unicorns... and most of the First Humanity. All this happened about sixty-five million years ago...

"The planet eventually recovered from what was then called the Great Cataclysm, the Great Flood... New species swarmed to replace those that had become extinct, and a Second Humanity—yours—finally arose from the ashes of the First to take over the Earth. However, not everyone and everything had perished during the Great Cataclysm. Strange beings had found refuge in the depths of the earth or under the oceans. Survivors of Mu and the last of the Danaians vowed not to repeat the mistakes of their predecessors and worked together to protect this new humanity, for it carried a great potential. That as the time of Atlantis and its thousand spires, a beacon of light in an otherwise still savage era...

"But Atlantis, too, fell. Some blame the monstrous Twilight Folk, who had come to Earth pursued by some mind-boggling enemy from the other end of the galaxy. The truth is shrouded in myths and legends. But in the wake of the Fall of Atlantis appeared the Immortals— my people.

"Our own records are not entirely clear about our origins. Some say we're bastard children of Fomores and Men; others, survivors of Mu; or the result of mysterious experiments conducted by the Danaians to prolong their race... As our name indicate, we do not age and can live forever, although we can be killed. We all have various psionic powers, just like mine: telepathy, telekinesis, illusion casting, energy manipulation, metabolic control, etc. etc., etc. In addition, the legacy of Atlantis enabled my people to master an array of advanced technology which was often mistaken for magic by the primitive people of the Second Humanity...

"The Immortals split into many groups who spread all over the Earth. They were soon revered as gods and often became the gods and goddesses of your various pantheons. As you probably guessed already, I belong to a clan of Immortals who settled in Ancient Egypt and lived in the splendid city of Heliopolis..."

Here, Ra paused. The other Hexagoneers were suspended to each of his words. He smiled, reassured by their reactions so far.

"It's... it's a pretty confusing version of world history," remarked the Dark Flyer.

"Some in the magical community have known most of this for a long time," remarked Rakar. "There are still denizens of Atlantis walking the Earth today."

"Our encounter with Ghool taught us that," said Cendrine.

Blackie Sullivan said nothing, but he thought of the Soul of Levan the Fomore, and the Martian origins of his powers...

"The Kalevala legends of my people bear troubling similarities to what Ben has just told us," Jukka said.

"It is true that some ethnologists hypothesize that the gods of our myths are nothing more than evolved beings using some forms of advanced science," added the Black Flyer.

As a man of science, he had to rationalize the concept of a world populated by gods and demons that had thrived when men were still mastering fire, especially since no concrete evidence of such stories had ever been found.

"At least we now know our friend Ben's true origins," said Cendrine. "But there's still something that I don't understand. You say you're one of the Immortals of Egypt, OK, but what about your pretty blonde face with blue eyes... And your parents...?"

"What if we let him finish?" the Mysterious Archer interrupted. "I think Ben was just at the beginning of his revelations."

Ra nodded.

"Thank you, Jukka. But you're right, Cendrine. This brings us back to my own story, which is somewhat convoluted, but it will help you understand who I am and why I am here today. You should also know that many of the events I'm going to tell you have been pieced together from third party accounts.

"It is hard for me to tell you about the glory of almighty Heliopolis. Imagine a futuristic city as the science-fiction illustrators of the last century pictured it, with tall spires and wide avenues, a city whose inhabitants fly through the air and devote their time to the arts and sciences. Picture in your mind pyramids with electronic circuitry flowing with silver energy like veins through a body; cyclopean temples with massive touch-sensitive pillars; palaces so grand that they look as if they were built to house titans... Heliopolis is the city of the gods; I can hardly call it otherwise.

"Great Aru was the one who led his clan of Immortals to the banks of the Nile... In this blessed land, under a benevolent sun, he founded Heliopolis, built in a few months thanks to psionic powers and advanced science. It was kept wisely out of sight of the humans who already thrived in Egypt. From it, Aru reigned for many centuries, and his influence allowed Egyptian civilization to rise and become the dominant empire in that part of the world.

"Aru had two sons: I, Ra, the elder, and Set, my younger brother. Then the time came when, tired of his responsibilities, our father decided to retire. He abdicated in my favor, and on that day, I went from being a carefree prince to a king in charge of an empire. I understood what the life of great Aru had been like and swore to prove myself worthy of his trust. Alas, Set could not bear to not inherit the throne, he who had been consumed by a devouring ambition for so long. He gathered supporters, including thrice-accursed Athor, and fomented a coup.

"I was then at the height of my glory, with powers vastly superior to mine today. I was the most powerful representative of a race far superior to Humanity; I was immortal, nearly invulnerable. Set knew this, of course, and envied me. He went looking for forbidden knowledge, seeking something powerful enough to kill an Immortal. And he found it in what we called the Realm of Shadows—a region between, an afterlife for the souls of those Immortals who have been destroyed by a spiteful fate. It is a barren spiritual plane, a grim landscape as far as the eye can see, fetid swamps, dead forests, a desert made of black sand... A powerful entity known as Etarr the Inevitable reigns over this deadly realm. The Seven Ghosts are said to reside there, as well; ghosts who, according to legends of my people, know the answers to all the mysteries of the universe...

"By some mysterious means, Set managed to enter and return alive from the Realm of Shadows, a virtually unheard of feat and one that speaks volumes about his determination to kill me. There he met the Seven Ghosts who told him the forbidden secret: how to utterly destroy even the most powerful of Immortals. Armed with this evil knowledge, he put his plan into action, but not without testing it first...

"It was then that my father passed away. Everyone in Heliopolis—myself included—thought that great Aru had died in battle against a cosmic threat, protecting Egypt and the world. He was given a sublime funeral, the homage of an entire people to the most glorious king who had ever lived. His body was embalmed and buried at the center of the Pyramid of the Sun, at the very heart of the city that he had built and which would for all eternity bear witness to his kindly reign. It was only later that I discovered the awful truth: Set had killed our father, committing the greatest crime that a man can be guilty of. He had taken advantage of Aru's retirement to strike a fatal blow using the weapon that the Seven Ghosts had allowed him to take. The success of his abominable scheme only comforted his ambition and he then put his primary project in motion, regicide after parricide...

"Still grieving over my father's passing, I saw nothing coming. All I remember is Set's hateful gaze and an excruciating pain as he plunged an obsidian dagger engraved with symbols older than time itself into my heart. And so I died at the hands of my brother...

"My presence here, among you, is of course proof that my story didn't end then and there. I was told what ensued much later, because I could hardly have been a direct witness. Once more, Heliopolis prepared to bury its king. But as my body was being prepared for embalming, the captain of my guard, the valiant Kaor, noticed the strange shenanigans of a few soldiers whom Set had corrupted; the villain wanted to make sure that my soul, too, was destroyed. So my friend fled from Heliopolis with my remains and ultimately gave his life to take them to the only person who could save me from this final death: the wise Tho, one of our most eminent scientists who had chosen to live like a hermit outside the city.

"Using his formidable science, Tho prevented my soul from escaping into the Realm of Shadows and instead hid it in the body of Lydia, his human servant, who became the very distant ancestor of my mother of Ben Leonard.

"Even though my physical body was gone, Set wasn't certain that he'd gotten rid of me for me. But eventually, he came to believe it and seized the throne of Heliopolis. He then began a reign of terror, subjecting the Immortals to his tyrannical rule. His plan was to conquer the world and he forced my people to forge new, abominable weapons in order to succeed with his demented plan. Accustomed to a peaceful life devoted to the arts, the Immortals suffered under his cruel yoke, but eventually they rebelled.

"Led by Osir, one of my father's faithful advisers, and General Anhur, they overthrew the tyrant, but Set was never more dangerous than when he was cornered. He used one of these new weapons to turn the entire population of Heliopolis to stone—in reality, a state of metabolic stasis. Then my accursed brother disappeared from the history of the world, and no one knew where he was, or what he did…

"Meanwhile, Tho's Lydia lived her life amongst the humans, watching over the Soul of Ra. She had many children, who in turn bore sons and daughters and so forth for nearly three millennia. With each generation, one of her offsprings was chosen to carry the precious burden. I am the last descendant of this brave mortal woman.

"I became Ra around the time Hexagon was formed. I regained some of my Immortal powers and memories. I soon found out that Set had returned and had managed to locate my soul, which at the time was still dormant within my body. Naturally, my brother was determined to kill me. Fortunately, Tho, who had managed to escape the fate of the other Immortals of Heliopolis, had been watching. He and his daughter, Anubi, prevented Set from murdering me, and eventually, they revealed my true nature to me. Alas, that came at the cost of his life, for Set, desperate to prevent my return, found a way to kill the old scientist's life. But this time, he'd been too late. With some friends, I had traveled to Egypt to find out what was happening to me. There, some of my psionic powers returned when I had to fight Set, but my memories of Heliopolis still remained mostly inaccessible.

"After many more adventures, I finally found the city and there, a device called the Vessel of Memory completed my transformation from Ben Leonard into Ra, rewriting my genetic code and restoring all of my memories. From then on, Ben Leonard and Ra were one and the same. I could fight Set on an equal footing. After a final battle, I succeeded in freeing my people from their petrification and restored them to life. Heliopolis became once more the glorious city of the Egyptian Immortals.

"However, I could not bring myself to sit on the throne again, because I knew Set was still free to commit more atrocities. So I entrusted Heliopolis into the hands of wise Osir and returned to the world of humans, first as Ben Leonard, journalist, then as Ra, a superhero.

"The fact that no one has ant files on me is because most of my past adventures have taken place off Earth in some strange dimensions. Set was so enraged that I had survived that he sought allies to bring me down. I had to pursue him through time and space, even meeting 'cousins' from other clans of Immortals. At some point, Set tried to get rid of me by killing one of my ancestors, but after that failed too, he traveled further back in time to try to murder Tho before he could save my soul. He even cast me into the Realm of Shadows where he hoped I would remain a prisoner forever, but I escaped from the clutches of Etarr the Inevitable and returned to Earth.

"Thanks to the help of a couple of loyal friends, Pipp and Lucy, I managed to defeat all the traps that my evil brother tirelessly set for me. Finally, after a mighty battle, I thought I had finally prevailed and would be able to enjoy some well-deserved rest in Heliopolis. But Osir warned that Set was not dead, as I had mistakenly thought, and was plotting in secret...

"This is the real reason why I joined Hexagon. It seems I had been unable to defeat my brother alone, so I thought that, by enlisting the help of powerful allies, I would be able to put an end to his evil schemes forever.

"Now you know the whole truth, as strange as it may seem to you. I hope you won't reject me take because my people need you—I need you."

The Hexagoneers were dazed after listening to Ra's story. The Immortal had used his telepathy to share images from his past with them. They had seen the spires of Heliopolis; they had heard Set's evil laugh; they had felt the cold winds of Valhalla where Ra had fought the Frost Giants alongside Thor and Loki; they had tasted the miasmas of the Realm of Shadows; and they had felt their hearts swell with joy when the Egyptian Immortals had long last been freed from their stasis...

There was no doubt in their minds that Ben had told them the truth and nothing but. His tale had revealed a part of Earth's past that had remained obscure until now. They understood why Ra had not told them all this when he had first joined: it was too much—even for them, who had walked on alien soils and trod other dimensions... But now, they had evidence, and more than that, they had a hint about the formidable threat they were about to face.

"Thank you for your, er, candor, Ben," said Black Lys, who was the first to tear herself away from their shared experience. "So now, we know who we're up against: your brother Set and his allies. But his goals remain unclear."

"True, but only up to a point," Rakar said. "Ben just told us that Set seeks to rule over the world. Now, we have confirmed that he has access to advanced transdimensional technology, likely stolen from Zhud. What we don't know is, what does he hope to accomplish with it—other than staging brutal and uncoordinated assaults like that attack on New York."

"We do know one more thing," added the Mysterious Archer. "Set is trying to assemble the Gateway of the Gods. What else do you know about it, Ben? What's its purpose?"

Ra froze. Even though he had become an Immortal again, some of his most ancient memories remained confused. While he remembered his life as Prince of Heliopolis, other things were but jumbled fragments in his mind. His knowledge of archaeology often mixed with Ra's actual remembrances and it was difficult for him to separate the two. However, telling his story had made his mind clear and sharper for the moment, and after a few seconds, he found the answer to the Archer's question.

"Yes, the Gateway of the Gods..." he murmured. "It was an artifact that my father built to allow the mortal Pharaohs to visit him. It is a direct portal to Heliopolis..."

He looked up, feeling the memories flooding in. His teammates stared at him in silence, waiting for the next revelation.

"When I liberated Heliopolis, I also banished Set. The dimensional barrier that now surrounds the city is set to detect and repel my brother. It will recognize his psionic signature. He can never set foot in Heliopolis again."

Dominik Nero was scrolling through a bunch of schematics on a tablet. A worried crease appeared on his forehead.

"Judging from what your brother retrieved from Melanos' base, he will be able to increase the power of your Gateway to travel between universes," he said without looking up from his screen. "No matter how strong your barrier is, he will be able to defeat it."

"So the attack on New York was just a warm-up," said Cendrine.

Ra stood up, an icy sweat running down his back.

"If Set plans to invade Heliopolis," he said, "the entire world in in peril."

CHAPTER VIII
The City of the Gods

The Hexajet tore through the Egyptian skies with a thunderous roar, leaving behind a white trail and the deafening echo of its supersonic engines. Hexagon had not left immediately for Egypt after Ra's revelations because the Dark Flyer had insisted on running a few tests with the Immortal to calculate the exact resistance of his telekinetic force field, in order to evaluate Amon's power. He was the only foe unknown to Ra and they needed to learn more about him.

The readings they obtained were nothing short of terrifying. Amon was as strong as Blackie Sullivan, making him one of the most powerful superhumans on Earth. And Set had other fearsome allies... Athor and Bastet were not to be underestimated. Plus, he was probably hiding other secret assets up his sleeve, like the Xans... Hexagon had to plan their next move accordingly.

The Dark Flyer had decided to wear his latest combat armor, an impressive hexagonium suit equipped with state-of-the-art weaponry. The Mysterious Archer had selected a veritable arsenal of special arrows with effects as varied as they were unexpected. Rakar had researched his most powerful spells and his face was adorned with mystic war paint that increased both his strength and his speed. Blackie Sullivan was eager to go *mano a mano* with Amon, a foe against whom he could give free rein to his power. As for Black Lys, she was as supremely confident as ever in her considerable power and abilities...

With all their preparations completed, Hexagon took off from New York in the direction of Egypt.

In the cockpit, the Dark Flyer and Rakar sat at the controls, flying the aircraft towards Heliopolis, according to the GPS coordinates provided by Ra. In the middle part of the Hexajet, the other members and Sweet had gathered. The young prodigy with the diaphanous skin had insisted on coming, much to Dominik's chagrin. But a millennia-old city inhabited by god-like beings was too much of a prize to be ignored. Dominik had finally surrendered to Sweet's demands, much to the amusement of his teammates, who had never seen him get the better of her in an argument.

Ra was presently drawing a holographic map of Heliopolis so that the other Hexagoneers could familiarize themselves with the topology of the city. As its former king, he knew the place very well, but revisiting it now required great concentration. He scrupulously drew all the avenues, the buildings, and the various levels. Leaning forward, Blackie Sullivan analyzed the plan as it materialized in three dimensions above the meeting table. He rubbed his chin pensively.

"It's going to be tough to defend your city," he said, pointing to several sectors. "It was clearly not designed to withstand major attacks. No walls, wide boulevards, no air defenses..."

"The original architects of Heliopolis had nothing to fear from invasion," Ra retorted. "The city lies in an adjacent mirrorverse of Egypt, impossible for any human invader to reach. Moreover, we, Immortals, are a peaceful people—normally..."

Blackie Sullivan grunted and groaned in his chair, looking unconvinced.

"It doesn't matter anyway," said Black Lys. "If the Xans materialize above the city or in its streets, like they did in New York, then most traditional defenses would be effectively useless."

Ra nodded. Next to him, the Mysterious Archer was recording the map of Heliopolis with superhuman acuity.

"All the same, Ben, I'm not sure why you needed us for this battle," Sweet interjected. "You're quite powerful yourself, and in this city, there are... how many more like you, ready to defend it?"

"About five hundred," replied Ra.

"Another five hundred of your kind, with psionic powers and superior tech... What do you have to fear?"

Ben sighed.

"I know this is difficult for you to understand," he explained, "but you must strive to think like us, beings with unlimited life expectancy, whose long lives rotate. Mostly around arts and sciences, never having had anything to fear from humans. Heliopolis is a supremely peaceful civilization. My people know almost nothing about war and have never used their powers aggressively. It was up to me, and me only, to fight their battles on Earth and elsewhere—that is my role as king. Except for Set's reign of terror, and the brief revolt that ensued, they have known nothing but peace."

Ra looked at each of his teammates in turn to give his words more weight. Black Lys and Sweet seemed convinced, but Blackie Sullivan still carried some doubt in his jet-black eyes. As for the Archer, he was as inscrutable as ever.

"Besides, not all Immortals are equal in psionic powers," Ben added. "Because of our ancestry, Set and I are amongst the most powerful; few others are on our level. Some Immortals hear plants think, others can use

104

their emotions to create rainbows of psychic light, some can read the past of an object by merely touching it... All of these abilities are useless in combat... Plus, they are not trained to fight. I hope you can see now why I need your help to defeat Set."

"So you're the only Immortal, besides your brother and his three cronies, who knows how to use his powers in battle?" asked Blackie Sullivan, still skeptical.

"Not quite. We do have a small guard selected from among those of us with suitably offensive powers. This, er, militia is led by General Anhur, whom I'm not even sure I could defeat in single combat if we ever had to face each other."

"I'm bothered by the fact that we have no real idea what forces Set has at his disposal," the Mysterious Archer said. "What if the Xan fleet that attacked New York was but a fraction of his resources? Also, for all we know, the three Immortals we fought in Boston are not the only ones siding with him."

Black Lys stood with her arms folded, contemplating the holographic representation of Heliopolis and trying to anticipate their enemy's actions. As leader of Hexagon, she already had several battle plans in mind and was always trying to be one step ahead. But here, she had too little to prepare adequately. She would have to rely on her instincts and improvise in the heat of the moment.

"Target in sight; we're almost there," Dominik's voice crackled on the intercom. Then, jokingly, he added: "Ladies and gentlemen, please fasten your seat belts, we're starting our descent towards Heliopolis. I hope you had a pleasant flight with Hexagon Airways!"

Sweet raised her eyes, shook her head, but couldn't repress a smile.

105

The Hexajet had, in fact, landed near the city of Luxor, not far from Mount Zefidu where, according to Ra, was the gate that would take them to Heliopolis. The Hexagoneers had equipped themselves to the best of their ability and followed their newest teammate through a rocky corridor that went under the mountain.

The searchlights on the Dark Flyer's armor swept the space in front of them so that they didn't blindly march through this underground maze of tunnels and caves.

The more they progressed, the more Rakar felt the presence of mystic fields. In this place, old magic was still strong, threatening to overwhelm even his mystical senses. He had always suspected that Ra carried within him the essence of the ancient world, when sorcery still reigned supreme—the Age of the First Humanity, when gods and demons walked among men. The young Lakota was now facing this reality and about to enter an unknown dimension where magic and science coinhabited.

Finally, Ra stopped in front of a rocky wall of cyclopean proportions. With a practiced gesture, he put his hand on it and turned towards his companions.

"My friends, welcome to Heliopolis!"

Suddenly, the wall disappeared and ahead and below them, the Hexagoneers beheld a city like no other. Grandiose in its architecture and in its dimensions, it stretched as far as the eye could see in a green valley where a river with waters as blue as the purest of sapphires lazily meandered. The azure sky was strewn with scattered clouds and adorned with a bright sun whose warm rays were bathing this idyllic landscape. Like an enchanted jewel in a beautiful setting, Heliopolis glowed in the midst of all this.

Almost unconsciously, the Hexagoneers stepped forward in the direction of this hypnotic scenery, setting off on a path down the hill.

As they got closer, they could make out the details of the city and, when they finally reached its gates, they were breathless. Heliopolis was impossible to describe. Ra had tried; he had even shared mental images of it with his companions; but none of that had prepared them to the moment when they actually walked along its avenues under the indifferent gaze of buildings several thousands of years old.

Everything here breathed power. The architecture combined Ancient Egyptian with futuristic designs. The buildings were titanic, piercing the very Heavens without defying them, rising respectfully towards the infinite. The city had been built on several levels, connected by walkways and anti-gravity elevators. Large, richly ornamented terraces offered a majestic panorama to the casual stroller. The marble-paved streets were almost supernaturally clean, strewn with fine sand that the wind blew from the banks of the river below. Scattered throughout this breathtaking scenery were parks and gardens, oases of nature in this wonder of glass and metal. They contained rare essences, whose spicy scents flattered the senses. Crystal fountains spouted in the midst of these miniature edens, while ponds and canals caught the sunlight and transformed it into iridescent rainbows.

Ra had described Heliopolis as the city of the gods, and that was indeed what it was.

As for the Immortals, they were everywhere, going about their business. They levitated, drove silent vehicles, sculpted, painted, and played music; they read on sunny terraces, played chess, and debated in sublime forums. They were as majestic and awe-inspiring as their city. They looked like ancient Egyptians dressed in togas adorned with intricate micro-circuitry and precious jewels enhancing their natural beauty. They all seemed serene.

As Ra walked by, they bowed and called him "my liege" exhibiting little or no surprise at his presence. The hero responded to their tributes with a wave of his hand and a soothing smile.

The personality of Ben Leonard began fading as that of Ra grew during their journey through Heliopolis. The Immortal became himself again among his people. Here, he was the king. It was his duty to protect his subjects and he knew they were in great danger. But he had returned accompanied by the world's greatest heroes. Surely, with their help, he was certain to triumph. The thought made him feel stronger.

Following Ra, the Hexagoneers finally arrived in front of the Palace of the Sun, the heart of and seat of power in Heliopolis. The men guarding the entrance lowered their heads as Ra approached and moved aside to let their king pass with his friends.

"His Excellency the Regent Osir awaits you in the council chamber, Your Highness," informed one of them.

They then crossed the immense palace gates.

Osir was a giant with a long white beard and a soft gaze, dressed in a large, immaculate toga and with a pharaonic crown sitting on his head. His eyes sparkled with joy as he saw Ra and the two Immortals gave each other a fraternal hug. Other dignitaries stood in the council chamber; all shared the same features and hieratic appearance that made them look like Ancient Egyptians. The Dark Flyer pointed out humorously that Ben with his blond hair, blue eyes and western looks stood out amongst his people like a cat at a dog show. But the Immortals saw beyond outward appearances; their superhuman senses perceived the psychic essence of their interlocutors. Thus, Ra's soul appeared to them in all its splendor, despite being housed in the body envelope of a mere human.

"My King!" exclaimed the Regent. "How good to see you again after these long years."

"It is a shared pleasure, Osir, my friend," replied Ra. "I wish, however, it were under more auspicious circumstances. It is bad news that bring me back to Heliopolis."

Osir nodded with visible concern; he motioned that they should sit at the marble table in the council chamber. Crystal glasses filled with wine and baskets of dried fruit were immediately brought in.

"First, let me introduce you to my friends," Ra said. "In the Outside World, these are known as Hexagon. They are a group of heroic mortals who have dedicated their lives to protect our world against some of its greatest threats. This is the Black Lys, their leader, whose fencing skills would put Anhur himself to shame; the Dark Flyer, master of machines, and his companion, the beautiful Sweet, whose mind has no equal; Blackie Sullivan, who commands the most fundamental forces of the cosmos; Rakar, wielder of the magic of his ancestors; and finally, the Mysterious Archer, whose fighting prowess and skills are known to wreak havoc on a battlefield.

"My friends, this is Osir, my father's most faithful adviser, whom I made Regent when I was forced to leave Heliopolis."

"It is an honor for our city to welcome such brave heroes within its walls," the Immortal replied with deep and sincere respect.

Each Hexagoneer had bowed slightly as they were introduced in turn, but they all felt a little uncomfortable in this environment that was beyond anything they had encountered before. Dominik, however, did not hesitate for long before tasting the scarlet wine that had been so kindly offered.

"I thought I heard my name!" thundered a voice from the entrance.

A man of colossal stature had come in and made his way in great strides towards Ra. He wore a heavy armor with silvery reflections, along, red cape, and a large, curved sword hung from his belt.

Before anyone could react, he lifted Ra in his arms , caught him in a bear hug, and burst out with a sonorous laugh that made the walls of the room tremble.

"You are back at last!" he said in a voice like thunder. "With promises of glory and honor, I hope?"

"I will tell you when you could stop trying to break my back," replied Ra, breathlessly.

The mighty Immortal deposited him on the ground and looked at the gathered group of heroes with a broad smile.

"This is General Anhur, of whom I told you earlier," said Ra. "He leads the most valiant of our warriors."

Anhur's gaze evaluated each member of Hexagon in turn, his appreciative eye lingering on the Black Lys. He made a deep curtsy to her.

"My beautiful lady, I do not know if your sword would pierce my heart, as my King said, perhaps a mite too rashly, but certainly, your incomparable beauty would, and against it I would know not how to defend myself."

Cendrine smiled. She often frequented the high society of Europe where attempts at seduction were as frequent as often as embarrassing. However, despite her best judgment, she liked the frank manners of this armored colossus.

"Enough, General," Osir admonished him. "Our King is the bearer of most sinister news and we are gathered here not to flirt but to take the full measure of the danger that hangs over Heliopolis."

With a sigh, the general sat down on a chair, which almost folded under his weight; he took a glass of wine and swallowed it in one gulp.

"Thank you, my friend," said Ra with a smile that quickly vanished. "I am indeed the bearer of bad news. As our soothsayers predicted, Set has returned. Unsurprisingly, he plots to retake Heliopolis. But this time, to further his goals, he has gathered an alien army. He is working with allies both old and new—Athor and Bastet, but also a mighty warriors called Amon…"

Anhur winced a little when the name of the beautiful Bastet was mentioned, but made no remarks.

"Whatever forces Set has gathered, Heliopolis is forever forbidden to him," Osir stated.

"Alas, I fear he may have found a way to break the barrier we erected against him. It appears he has found the Gateway of the Gods."

A murmur spread throughout the room.

"Let your accursed brother dare to show his face in Heliopolis! I have a score to settle with him!" thundered Anhur, striking the table with his fist. "It's been too long since he's escaped my wrath."

"Well said," agreed several of the other Immortals.

111

"It seems as if the battle is inevitable," said Black Lys. "So we just have to prepare for it as best we can."

Everyone nodded in agreement.

"Nevertheless, we mustn't underestimate Set," said Ra. "He is wily and powerful. That is why I brought Hexagon here..."

"My King, with all due respect to your mortal allies, this is a war between Immortals," interrupted Anhur.

"Not anymore, General," said Black Lys. "Set has attacked one of our cities; he has gone after those we are sworn to protect. It is our duty to stop him."

"Besides," added Rakar, "if he wins here, if Heliopolis falls, the entire Earth will be in danger."

Anhur harrumphed but did not contradict the Hexagoneer.

"We are in agreement," concluded Ra. "The city must be placed on high alert. All defenses must be activated."

"Thy will be done, O My King," approved Osir. "General Anhur, mobilize the troops."

The General saluted, then left the room as he had entered it, loudly shouting orders before he had even got through the door.

"I like this guy," Dominik joked.

After elbowing him in the ribs, Sweet stood up, a little embarrassed.

"Mister, er, Regent," she said hesitatingly as she showed him the computer she carried around with her, "I have all the data on Set's forces here... the Xans and all that..."

Ra smiled at Osir's uncomprehending expression.

"It's not necessary, Sweet," he explained. "As soon as we arrived, I used my powers to transfer all the information into the memory of Atum, the great computer of Heliopolis. Any Immortal here is now able to access it telepathically."

"Wow!" exclaimed the young prodigy. "You'll have to teach me that trick!"

"I promise, but first, I have one last thing to show you all."

Ra again guided his teammates through the streets of Heliopolis. This time, they moved away from the busy center to go to the outskirts where reigned a strange calm because no one lived there.

The Immortal led the Hexagoneers past an austere-looking building, a grayish bunker that contrasted sharply with the magnificence of the rest of the city. This colossal stone cube was set in the middle of a vast field surrounded by thick ramparts. It radiated a foreboding sense of menace, and every Hexagoneer felt his hair stand up as they approached it.

The high doors of that bunker opened as Ra approached and the interior lit up with pale lights. A long corridor led deep into the bowels of the Earth. The Immortal beckoned his companions to follow him. As they descended through this tunnel, no one uttered a word. The atmosphere was too overwhelming and stifled any desire for a conversation.

Finally, after what seemed to be an endless journey, the Group arrived in a dark room of overwhelming proportions, so huge that it seemed as if it could contain an entire city. On either side of the entrance were two granite statues of muscular men more than seven feet tall. As Ra approached, these sculptures began to glow and come to life.

"Welcome back, O King of Kings!" said a deep voice, whose echo reverberated around the room.

And the statues bowed before Ra.

"These are the Nega-men," said the Immortal. "Androids that I designed myself to protect this place."

"And what is this place exactly?" asked Black Lys, unable to repress a shiver.

Ra had a contrite smile.

"I told you the Immortals are a peaceful people. But that hasn't stopped our scientists from building many weapons, each more powerful than the next, some even capable of shattering a planet. This is our Arsenal."

"Ah!" Blackie Sullivan exclaimed. "I thought your story sounded much too good to be literally true. Immortal or not, man cannot change his nature."

"And yet, Fred, I only told the truth. To my shame, I confess that I myself created most of these artifacts of destruction, but I always did it with the intention of protecting my people, even though this seems like a weak excuse today. Many more were forged by Set when he briefly sat on the throne of Heliopolis..."

Ra made a gesture and all the lights came on at once. Mighty and deadly-looking machines stretched as far as the eye could see, radiating an aura of palpable danger. There were cannons capable of splitting a planet, bombs powerful enough to extinguish stars, missiles filled with deadly, unknown viruses... Countless shelves were stocked with weapons more suitable for hand-to-hand combat, but which looked just as dangerous as the titanic killing machines that filled this room.

The Hexagoneers took a few steps into this strange armory. The Mysterious Archer examined some of the weapons with an expert eye. Ra took a small cylinder from a display and smiled with nostalgia. The Dark Flyer and Sweet went from one machine to another, their scientific curiosity proving stronger than their uneasiness.

"This is... incredible," said Dominik. "I've designed quite a few weapons myself, but what I see here is beyond even my imagination!"

Rakar, on the other hand, stayed away. The morbid atmosphere that reigned here weighed on him more heavily than the others. For a shaman, this was an uncomfortable and disturbing sensation. Black Lys, who somehow felt the same, put a hand on his shoulder and smiled reassuringly. The young Lakota tried to put on a brave face, but the icy sweat running down his back spoke volumes about the impact that the dreadful atmosphere of the arsenal was having on him.

"This is all very interesting," said Blackie Sullivan, "but why did you bring us here, Ben?"

"Isn't it obvious?" answered the Mysterious Archer before Ra could even open his mouth. "When Set attacks Heliopolis, one of his main objectives will undoubtedly be to seize control of this arsenal. He then will be able to force the city to surrender, under threat of using some kind of doomsday weapon stored here."

"And after that, he'll use some of that hardware to conquer the world," finished Black Lys. "I know you all felt it, just like Rakar and I did. To merely stand here is to be almost overwhelmed by the sheer power of total destruction that resides in this room. C.L.A.S.H., all the other superhumans... No one would be a match for these weapons."

A heavy silence greeted this somber statement.

"Alas, Cendrine is correct," said Ra. "If my brother seizes control of what is kept in this room, not just Heliopolis, but the world itself is doomed. The Nega-men

115

provide effective protection, because they emit a radiation they neutralizes our psionic powers, but as we have learned, Set has other cards up his sleeve."

"Such as the Xans," Dominik remarked. "I take it that your Nega-men have no effect on any beings other than you Immortals?"

"That's right," replied Ra. "They're strong and resilient, but Blackie Sullivan or you would easily be able to destroy them."

"That's why you need us," said the Mysterious Archer. "If this building is attacked, some of us will have to fight alongside your Nega-men, and we would have nothing to fear from them. Clever."

"Yes," Ra agreed. "Your primary task will be to prevent Set from taking control of this Arsenal while the army of Heliopolis repels the assaults of his troops."

"Why don't you use those weapons against your brother?" asked Blackie Sullivan. "If they're as powerful as you say..."

"I'm afraid our city wouldn't survive it, Fred, and probably neither would you," replied the Immortal. "The weapons are too powerful in inexperienced hands! Using them is a risk I'm not prepared to take. We'll have to defeat Set using our own resources."

"Can they be destroyed?" asked Rakar.

"Yes, but not easily, and I'm afraid we're already running out of time."

A light tube hanging on a wall then crackled before going out, casting a shadow on the face of the King of Heliopolis—not unlike an omen of doom.

CHAPTER IX
A Moment of Peace

While the visit to the Arsenal had put the Hexagoneers in a gloomy mood, the rest of the evening was fortunately much more enjoyable.

Osir had prepared a banquet to celebrate the return of his King. The heroes took their seats around a beautifully decorated table, loaded with dishes, each one more succulent than the last. The smell of these delicacies wetted everyone's appetite, and many Immortals were there to pay tribute to Ra and get to meet these heroic mortals whose reputation had already spread around the city.

General Anhur sat next to Cendrine and spent a good part of the evening regaling her with the story of her exploits and asking her questions about her adventures with Hexagon. The French woman appreciated the company; the General was quite a character, had a great sense of humor, and his interest in her was not feigned.

The Mysterious Archer and Rakar were engaged in a heated discussion with Sebek, one of the captains of the guards, whose face bore a pale scar under his right eye. They debated the merits of various strategies and compared their experiences on the battlefield. The conversation was lively, with laughter and admiring exclamations after one or the other had finished recounting a particularly remarkable exploit.

Dominik enjoyed the banquet; as a bon vivant, he tried every dish and tasted every alcohol with equal gusto. It was a real delight for him to be able to savor this exotic cuisine with its ancient flavors in such a sumptuous setting. Sweet had given up asking him to go easy; she herself had gotten her hands on Djehut, one of the scribes in charge of Atum, the central computer, and was peppering him with questions about its psychic interface, the existence of which had been revealed earlier by Ra. The youthful-looking Immortal did his best to provide her with intelligible answers; to his surprise, the beautiful young human female had managed to follow his explanations as if her mind could easily bridge the technological gap between Heliopolis and the rest of the world. Finally, she wrung from him the promise to show him the interface after the banquet.

Ra, who had been catching up with Osir, was delighted to see his teammates get along so well with his people. It was important for him to feel that they be considered as trusted friends and not just allies of convenience. The coming battle would demand a great deal of trust and solidarity.

The atmosphere of Heliopolis did wonders for the spirits of the Hexagoneers, bringing them a sense of calm before the battle. Osir had acted wisely in organizing this banquet, since breaking bread together strengthens alliances and brings soldiers closer. As he gently touched the minds of his teammates, Ra suddenly realized that Blackie Sullivan was not among them. He wasn't too surprised, however, because he knew that the master of dark matter was a loner who kept himself apart. While he had not known him when Blackie was, first, Max Tornado's arch-enemy, then one of Hexagon's fiercest foes, he knew that the former villain did not yet feel that he fully belonged with the team. He had fought alongside them, but did not yet share in their joys and sorrows. He still felt unworthy somehow.

Abandoning his train of thoughts, Ra returned to his conversation with Osir, trying not to be concerned. He knew that, when the time came, all his teammates would stand by his side.

The banquet had gradually come to an end and the guests were leaving. The night was already well advanced and Black Lys stood on the balcony of one of the reception rooms, overlooking the stunning gardens below. She was admiring the skyline of Heliopolis, its streets and buildings illuminated with so many colors. The city was calm, the view soothing, even in the midst of the darkness. In the sky above, the stars shone, cold and eternal.

General Anhur kept Cendrine company. After a playful conversation, they had fallen silent while the silver-haired swordswoman had become lost in her contemplation of Heliopolis.

"It's so beautiful," she whispered.

"The calm before the storm," grumbled Anhur, throwing his cape over her shoulders in a gallant gesture.

She thanked him with a smile.

"When do you think Set attack?" she asked.

"Soon enough, I'm afraid," replied the General. "According to you, he already has all his pieces in place; all he has to do now is make his first move. He knows that you are after him, since our King has already fought his henchmen. I won't be surprised if he shows up tomorrow."

Black Lys shivered. The peace that reigned over Heliopolis made that perspective seem so distant, absurd even... How could anyone want to desecrate such beauty, bring death and destruction to such a holy place?

"How do you fight him?" she asked.

Ra had, of course, described his past battles against his evil brother, but she needed to learn more.

"You led the rebellion against him... What kind of foe is he?"

Anhur thought for a moment. He hesitated because they were after all talking about his king's brother, but he decided to forget the protocols and be truthful.

"He's a sly one," he finally said. "Alas, he can hardly be called a coward because the mad ambition that drives him leads him to take all kinds of risks and try all kinds of schemes. He went into the Realm of Shadows, which is madness, murdered his father and tried to destroy his brother... He is devious, intelligent, and powerful enough to crush even the strongest minds. His natural charisma allows him to prey on the weak-minded and rally around him those who share the same evil dreams."

"You paint the picture of an enemy that will be most difficult to defeat," remarked Cendrine.

"Yes, Set is indeed formidable, and should never be underestimated, but he also has weaknesses. His hatred of Ra is one; it gnaws at him like an insidious and debilitating disease. It pushes him to make mistakes. More than once, he could have destroyed the King, but he was too eager to see him suffer first, and that, ultimately. led to his defeat. Another weakness is his pride..."

"I see. We fought enemies just like him—and won. Remind me to tell you about the Necromancer sometime... It's up to us to find the chink in his armor then. Thank you for your forthrightness, General."

Anhur bowed deferentially.

"You are most welcome, beautiful lady. Now I must leave you," he added regretfully. "I still have to check on our defenses and boost my men's spirits Enjoy this night while it lasts, Black Lys—and you may keep the cape."

Cendrine watched the General walk away with a sweet smile, then wrapped herself in the thick cloth. She returned to her contemplation of the city. Her mind was already thinking about how best to take advantage of the information she had just received if she ever found herself facing Set.

Suddenly, she perceived that she was no longer alone on the balcony.

"So?" she just asked.

Blackie Sullivan's dark silhouette stood out against the city lights.

"I've been around Heliopolis and talked to a few of the locals," he said with a shrug. "Ben was telling the truth: these Immortals have no idea about what might happen next. They have lived for too long in peace and have but very abstract notions of war. They were petrified for, like, three thousand years, so they live outside of time. Ra freed them and, since then, they feel only boundless admiration for him; the absolutely trust him. They know he has defeated Set many times before, and therefore they harbor no doubts about the issue of our battle... Lucky bastards!"

"That's not good," said Black Lys.

"No, it's not."

Blackie's face took on a harsh expression. Looking at it, Cendrine couldn't help but think of Jeff Sullivan, the previous leader of Hexagon and Blackie's deceased brother. They looked very much alike and suddenly, she was almost overcome by nostalgia. She idly wondered how different things would be if the so-called "Man of Brass" was leading them now. Despite Blackie's vas powers, she knew she would have felt more confident in the outcome of their battle. It was unfair to Fred, of course, who had proven himself in their fight against

121

Ghool, and whose good faith she didn't doubt for even a moment, but Jeff had the rare ability to inspire his teammates like no others. Blackie, on the other hand, was a lone wolf, not a leader... Still, she knew she could rely on him and his powers.

"Do you have a plan of action?" he asked her.

"Yes, but you may not like it," she replied, amused.

Fred grunted and nodded. Since joining Hexagon, he had respected Cendrine's authority and followed her orders without question, sometimes to the astonishment of his teammates who had been less than disciplined themselves. Blackie Sullivan had fought the stunning swordswoman before, when he had been a villain, and knew and respected her skills as a warrior and a strategist. His respect for a worthy opponent had since turned into admiration for a very effective leader.

"I think I can guess," he said. "You'll have me guard the Arsenal, right?"

"Yes. You're our last line of defense, in case the Immortals and Hexagon can't stop Set."

"What about the others?"

"The Archer and Rakar will try to cull the invaders from behind; that should make your task easier. The Dark Flyer will handle air support. I expect to see Xan Cruisers again. As for Ra, well, he'll be in charge of the Immortals. He'll be coordinating defenses with Anhur."

"I like the General," Blackie remarked. "If they were all like him, we wouldn't be needed."

They heard soft, dulcet tones emanating from the very walls of the palace, while silver petals danced in the air according to the melody.

"This is amazing place," said Blackie. "It reminds me a little of Orios."

"That's why we're going to protect it," said Black Lys with determination. "Come on, Fred, you should get some rest. The attack could happen at any time..."

"I know. And so should you, Cendrine."

Like Anhur had done earlier, Fred Sullivan walked away into the night. Left alone on the balcony, Lys couldn't suppress a shiver despite the General's cape wrapped around her shoulders. She took one last look at the lights of Heliopolis and then returned to the shelter of the palace walls.

CHAPTER X
The Battle Begins

The sun was barely above the horizon when the alarm sounded. Throughout Heliopolis, a muffled and repetitive sound, like that of a hammer striking a bronze gong, awoke the Immortals from their slumber.

The Hexagoneers, however, had been ready for a while. As soon as the alert sounded, Ra connected their minds telepathically. Although scattered throughout the city, all six heroes were in contact with each other, as well as Osir and Anhur.

The Black Lys stormed out of her luxurious bedroom, already outfitted for battle. All around her, frightened Immortals looked at her anxiously, waiting for orders. The swordswoman was the first to arrive at the palace square. There, she stood frozen before the spectacle that she beheld.

The sky had literally split in two, with a wide chasm in the middle opening towards... elsewhere. The rift widened until it covered the city from side to side. From it then emerged first ten, then fifteen, then twenty Xan vessels which positioned themselves above Heliopolis with a deafening roar. Cendrine recognized the characteristic flicker of their protective magnetic fields.

From the belly of the ships sprang antigravity tubes which dropped countless squads of the alien reptilians on the ground, ready to spread out in the streets to sow death. From the sides of the ships came fleets of two-seater hovercrafts which, like deadly insects, buzzed through the air and slalomed between the buildings in search of prey. Finally, from the rear of the vessels came light tanks with swiveling double-cannons which glided to the streets below in order to occupy strategic positions at the intersections.

Cendrine cursed in colorful French. The attack was massive; she had expected it, but had hoped that she had overestimated the size of Set's army. The Xans were mercenaries; she idly reflected that their foe must have broken the bank to hire so many of them.

Above her, she saw the massive shape of the Dark Flyer in full battle mode with armored wings and laser cannons fly over. Behind her, Ra and General Anhur had just arrived.

She began to issue orders telepathically.

"Dark Flyer, try to limit their bombardment capabilities and shoot down everything you can. Rakar, Archer, defend the city perimeter, especially the streets leading to the Arsenal. You won't stop them all, but Blackie will take care of the rest..."

"I sure will," answered the master of dark matter. *"I'm already in position; in fact, I slept here."*

Black Lys allowed herself a smile.

"Excellent! Ra, keep this communication channel open. And do your best. You know the enemy. This is your city and your people. Be worthy of the title of King."

"Thank you, Cendrine," Ben replied.

Black Lys then turned towards Anhur.

"General," she said aloud, "if you would do me the honor...?"

The Immortal dressed in silver and bronze armor laughed fiercely and pointed his curved sword at the swarming mass of Xans now scattered throughout Heliopolis.

"Attack!" he shouted.

The soldiers, all armed and motivated, ran, flew, leapt, and teleported themselves at the enemy, echoing his cry.

Black Lys spread her arms open and from her open hands sprang two blades of bluish energy; they roared aggressively, as if eager to fight. Anhur looked at them with respect, then rushed after his men; she followed him, her right eye now adorned with her family crest.

In the skies above, the Dark Flyer was hunting Xans. The red eagle that adorned the chest of the dark armor he wore was a bird of prey, and at that moment, Dominik felt in synch with that symbol chosen by his father, the first Dark Flyer. The battle suit he wore was massive, yet mobile and fast. He needed that maneuverability, being chased by a dozen hovercrafts. The flying vehicles resembled antique tanks, driven by one Xan while another acted as a gunner. The laser bursts were flying all around him, but he dodged them with ease.

His attention was focused on the many alien vessels casting their ominous shadows over Heliopolis. He had to shoot down as many as possible, because they represented the most dangerous threat to the city. As he gained altitude, he was able to make a sudden turn around and attack the hovercrafts like a bird of prey. The Xans swerved as best they could, but the Dark Flyer struck mercilessly and with uncanny precision. The enemy's flying machines went down like so many partridges and crashed here and there on the ground or into buildings.

Having gotten rid of his irksome attackers, Dominik now flew at near supersonic speed towards an alien ship. He fired at it with his entire arsenal—missiles, lasers, high-velocity bullets... But the Xans' protective field held up, as he suspected it would. In response to his attack, a new swarm of hovercrafts came out of the vessel and began chasing him. He was hit several times, but the aliens had nothing that could pierce his hexagonium suit. Nevertheless, he retreated, feeling frustrated.

Suddenly, a squadron of soldiers from Heliopolis appeared. Some were flying, others just materialized out of thin air, standing on small, round energy disks; and a few more attacked by turning themselves into gas or energy.

The Dark Flyer gave them a quick but heartfelt salute. He was no longer alone in the sky: the Immortals were prepared to defend their city! They were not wearing uniforms or carrying weapons; they were merely citizens eager to help the outsider. Alas, the Xans were fierce and ruthless, and the hovercraft guns began mowing them down. Bodies crashed one after the other to the ground below. The aliens killed without remorse, and Dominik felt a boiling rage rising within him.

"I am the Dark Flyer!" he shouted. "I'm not afraid of you! Cowards! Come and face me!"

And he went wild: the lasers coming out of his gloved hands caused the hovercrafts to explode; the vertigo waves emitted by his armor disoriented the alien pilots who crashed; the bullets shooting out of his shoulder cannons mowed down the enemy... The Dark Flyer was giving the Xans a taste of their own medicine, but as more and more of them arrived, he decided to lure them to him rather than needlessly expose the Immortals.

However, he began to lose some of the hovercrafts in the maze that was Heliopolis. He himself was having trouble finding his way around.

"*Honey, can you hear me?*" suddenly said a familiar voice on his intercom.

"Sweet, is that you?" he replied.

"Who else, handsome? I'm with Djehut inside their, er, I guess you'd call it 'command center.' You should see it. Their computer, Atum... It's enough to revolutionize all modern computing..."

"I'm a little busy right now..."

"I know. I see you on my screen. That's why I called..."

Dominik suddenly saw various diagrams, plans and schematics scroll across the scarlet visor of his helmet.

"Call me your friendly neighborhood urban planner! I've just sent you the plan of the transformations I'm going to implement in the neighborhood you're passing through. I can order all of them from here by simply reprogramming Atum."

Dominik saw a three-dimensional map appear in the corner of his visor. It showed buildings, bridges and towers being literally rearranged around him. He could now anticipate these changes half a second before they occurred, unlike the hovercrafts chasing him, which proved fatal for the Xans A wall collapsed, a tunnel opened, a terrace retracted... in mere minutes, the configuration of the neighborhood had changed completely. The Dark Flyer was able to navigate this ever-changing environment thanks Sweet. He saw the Xans crash into a wall that wasn't there a moment before, being crushed by a new arch suddenly springing from the road, smash into a new bridge now connecting two terraces... He finished the job by shooting down the few survivors who hadn't been destroyed by these transformations.

"Well done, Sweet!" he enthused. "Do you have anything for an encore?"

"*I do! I spent the night learning new tricks from Djehut. This town has the potential to defend itself if we give it a little help...*"

"Can you get it to give me a hand with those ships?"

"*I think I can... See that golden pyramid to your left? Go to the top of it...*"

Dominik spotted the building, a Cyclopean construction whose four sides were dotted with dark panels that looked like circuitry and were crossed by crackling cables. He landed on it and clung to the aerial that sprang from its top. Suddenly, cables sprang up from all around him and connected to his armor.

"Hey! What are you doing?" he asked.

"*Don't worry. This is a power plant,*" explained Sweet. "*It runs on solar power and right now, it's at full capacity. Guess who's going to be able to draw from it?*"

As soon as Sweet had uttered these words, Dominik felt a power surge through every part of his battle suit. The energy flowed like liquid through his circuitry, filling his components with a power he had never experienced before. It was almost too much...

"*Knock yourself out!*"

Dominik directed this flow of new power to his chest. The scarlet eagle decorating it began to radiate an increasingly intense crimson light. The Dark Flyer took aim at one of the alien vessels and released the energy in a single, high-density beam, as red as a ruby. The ship's force field burst like a soap bubble; the crimson laser beam literally sliced the ship in half. The two sections of the alien vessel then exploded, scattering a fine rain of debris everywhere.

Without taking the time to savor his triumph, Dominik targeted another ship and fired again, destroying a second cruiser, then a third, then a fourth... His armor absorbed and transformed all the energy of Heliopolis—the very power of the Sun!—and struck mercilessly at the alien fleet, reducing its numbers considerably.

"Sweet?" he called.

"Yes?"

"I love you!"

Dominik could easily picture in his mind the smile that would light up his girlfriend's face.

The Mysterious Archer leapt to the side, barely taking the time to aim before releasing his arrows. Behind him, a wall was shattered by the laser beam from an enemy tank. But the armored vehicle did not have time to fire a second shot: the explosive arrow pulverized it and its wreckage added to that already sprawled along the avenue.

Rakar reached out to his partner to help him. Both were covered in dust and their uniforms were torn in places. They had been fighting for a long time without feeling as if they were really slowing down the Xans' advance. They were fighting on foot, using classic guerrilla tactics: ambush, escape, strike from afar, set traps...

The two heroes were assisted by a squad from the Heliopolis guards. They had spent a good part of the evening fraternizing with these men and their officer, Captain Sebek, playing dice while enjoying a delicious local wine. The camaraderie that they had forged had proved its effectiveness on the battlefield. The Immortals valued the Hexagoneers and obeyed their instructions. Alas, the Xans didn't lack for reinforcements and kept advancing through the city, opening up a path towards the Arsenal at the cost of its citizens' lives.

One block had already been lost and the next, where they presently fought, incorporated a major intersection that lay at the crossroads between the central district and the outskirts. For the time being, the Xans' attempts to break through had all been repelled thanks to the courage of a dozen guards. These Immortals had offensive psychic powers: one made spirals of fire appear and dance around before launching them at the enemy and incinerating him; another blew an arctic wind that froze the tracks of their tanks; and another could hurl a war cry that sent a shock wave at the aliens. As for Captain Sebek, he could slow down time around him and used this power to massacre entire legions of Xans who had become as motionless as statues.

The small squadron of defenders had retreated behind the shelter of a half-collapsed wall. Moving forward, Set's alien army was still approaching, just more cautiously than before.

"We can't hold out much longer," Rakar said, wiping the dust from his face.

"If we manage to stop that next phalanx, that will slow them down for a while," noted the Mysterious Archer. "The streets here are too narrow for their tanks. If we can immobilize them here, it'll take them a lot of time to get through. And we'll mow them down at will as they keep trying."

"Right. How do you suggest we do this?"

"Infiltration. We must create chaos in their ranks first. When they become disorganized, we can sweep in."

Sebek was crouching down beside the two Hexagoneers. He looked defeated.

"But I've just lost three more men," he said. "This position is untenable; we must retreat!"

"Give us one more chance, Captain," Rakar asked. "We can still turn this around. Let their sacrifice not be in vain."

The Lakota shaman stood up and drew new patterns on his face using the soot and dust that partially covered it. In a soft voice, he sang ancient words that belonged here, in this ageless city. The magic that resided in Heliopolis gave strength to his spell as if the city itself sensed his need and came to his help.

His silhouette began to blur and even the Mysterious Archer had to squint to see him. Rakar hadn't become truly invisible, but he blended into the background like a chameleon.

"Wait for my signal," he said.

He ran out of their shelter. In front of him, a tight formation of Xans on foot preceded four tanks. Rakar proceeded cautiously. A light wind lifted a cloud of dust around him. Shadows stretched out in front of him at unlikely angles. The Hexagoneer knew that the Xans could sense his body heat. He carried with him his two weapons of choice: his sacred tomahawk and his enchanted cutlass.

Without hesitation, Rakar leapt into the middle of the aliens when they came within reach. He struck and killed as many of them as possible, seeking to create terror among the Xans. They turned against each other, distinguishing only a fuzzy shape that crisscrossed their ranks. Shots were fired without hitting the hero; several aliens fell, struck by the bolts fired by their companions. Rakar kept sneaking between them, slitting a throat here, smashing a skull there, all the while blending into the background. In no time at all, the Xan formation descended into chaos as they searched in vain for their attacker.

With a grim smile, Rakar looked at his work. Then, with one stride, he climbed onto the roof of a tank. A Xan emerged from inside it. Rakar grabbed him by the neck and pulled him out before throwing him to the ground. Then he slipped inside the armored vehicle and stabbed its two drivers without giving them time to move. He settled at the controls after tipping a body over to take his place and pointed its cannon at the neighboring tank. Firing at close range shattered the other vehicle's armor and the infantrymen panicked even more.

"I guess that's the signal," said the mysterious Archer, smiling.

He rushed out of their shelter and, with just three paces, he had fired five explosive arrows at their enemies. Xan bodies were thrown into the air. Sebek gave the order to attack. The Hexagoneers and the Immortals stormed in and completed the destruction of the phalanx. Flames roared and melted the tracks of one tank; an arctic blast froze another. Xans seemed to move in slow motion as Sebek passed among them, his blade reddened with their blood…

The fight didn't last long. The Hexagoneers' tactics had paid off and the avenue was now littered with Xan bodies and the carcasses of their tanks. It was a barricade that would greatly slow down the troops to come.

As Rakar emerged from his tank, an alien ship exploded in the sky, then several others, one after the other.

"And unless I'm mistaken, that's the Dark Flyer's work!" said the Mysterious Archer.

Rakar smiled back. The battle was going well—so far.

The Black Lys' twin energy blades were dancing in her hands, mowing down any Xan who got too close to her. She was encouraged by the presence of Anhur at her side. The General was a superb warrior endowed with superhuman strength; his sword struck and killed five opponents at once. Together, the Immortal and the Hexagoneer had opened a wide breach in the enemy ranks at the landing point where most of the Xan forces were gathered, not far from the palace. Other Immortals had rushed into that breach and were now repelling the alien army.

Fighting back to back, Black Lys and Anhur experienced the unique pleasure felt by swordsmen when risking their lives in battle.

"My Lady, if we emerge victorious from this battle, I hope you will accept an invitation to dinner!" shouted the General as he slayed a colossal Xan.

"My General, if we get through this, you can have a permanent dinner invitation at my chateau," replied Cendrine, smiling, her swords slicing the weapons of one of her opponents.

"Ah! You have a chateau?"

"It's been in my family for a few centuries."

Suddenly, another voice broke in:

"Oh, my beloved, but a few centuries and already you forget me for another's pretty eyes?"

Bastet had appeared, perched high on a parapet watching the scene with his beautiful, green, mocking eyes, grinning like a panther about to lunge on her prey.

"Bastet!" roared the General. "You dare show yourself in my presence! You've forfeited any right to return to Heliopolis when you chose to ally yourself with foul Set and support his wicked schemes!"

Bastet stretched his supple body, barely dressed in a translucent toga, as if already tired of these recriminations.

"Yes, yes," she laughed. "Whatever excuses you need to tell yourself, lover. And you, mortal bitch," she spat, piercing Cendrine with her feline gaze, "take care not to rise too far above your condition!"

"The bitch is ready," replied the swordswoman, executing a salute with her blades. "By the way, honey, how is your cheek?"

Bastet put a hand to her perfect face, right on the spot where, a few days earlier, the Mysterious Archer had struck her with a rifle butt. She hissed back in anger.

Anhur suddenly leaped towards her, demonstrating a speed and an agility that one would not have suspected in someone of his bulk. But Bastet was even faster. Nimble as a cat, she hit the General with her claws, barely missing his eyes, then pulled out her own sword. The Immortal in silver armor threw himself into the fight with fury, and Bastet responded with equal passion; it was like an echo of their former passion.

Sensing that the duel between these two could drag on for a long time, the Black Lys decided to take over from Anhur and gave instructions to the guards to secure the cleared perimeter and cut off access to all roads leading to the palace. It had become quickly apparent that it was one of Set's main targets.

Out of the corner of her eye, she suddenly realized the extent of Bastet's treachery: while the feline Immortal was keeping the General occupied, behind him several Xans had taken position. They aimed at Anhur and fired. The silver armor shattered in several places under the effect of the rays. The General shouted with surprise as well as pain. Thus distracted, he couldn't see Bastet jumping on him. Her claws plowed his chest and spilled his blood.

"Curses!" cried the Immortal. "What cowardice is this?"

"You have always confused courage with stupidity, lover," whispered the feline Immortal.

As Anhur knelt down, she raised a hand to deliver the *coup de grâce*. But an energy blade stopped her and then forced her to step back. The Black Lys stood in front of her, her right eye burning with cold flame, in a fighting stance.

"The General is too gallant to strike a woman down," she said, "but I have no such scruples."

"You're insane, you mortal bitch," spat the Immortal. "You stand no chance against me!"

"Wanna bet?"

The Hexagoneer, displaying superior fighting skills, quickly forced Bastet back. The two women circled around each other, looking for a break. The Immortal leapt first, tearing the air with her claws. Black Lys dodged, then counterattacked. The green-eyed warrior was fast, which made up for her more rudimentary technique. Nevertheless, Cendrine had to deploy all her skills, only managing to avoid her dazzling attacks with considerable difficulty.

Meanwhile, in the sky above, several cruisers exploded noisily.

"Black Lys!" shouted Anhur, now surrounded by Xans. "Take care... I'm coming!"

"No need, General!" replied Cendrine as Bastet's claws drew scarlet furrows in her left arm. "I have this under control. Take care of the ships on the ground. They keep pouring out troops! Find a way to stop them!"

The Immortal nodded with regret. Overwhelmed by his opponents, he called upon his troops to rally around him. Guards rushed forward and used their powers to rescue their leader. The Xans were variously struck by lightning, turned to stone, swept by a swirling wind...

Finally free, Anhur drove his sword into the ground. He took a deep breath and looked up at the massive ship casting its shadow over the battlefield. His hands tightened and two balls of concentrated psychic energy—pure mental plasma—appeared within them. With a scream, the General threw them towards the cruiser which was engulfed in a cataclysmic explosion. The debris were thrown hundreds of yards away as a cloud of flame and smoke rose up into the heavens. On the ground, the fighting stopped for a moment after this masterful feat.

Black Lys felt a shiver of fear run through her as she watched this demonstration of sheer power. Even Bastet appeared shaken. When she saw Anhur create two new spheres of destruction, she rushed towards him to stop him, but the Hexagoneer got in her way again.

"Oh, no, honey, you're not going anywhere!" she exclaimed.

And their ballet resumed, dazzling attacks against skillful parries, a human trained since birth against an Immortal with superhuman agility and speed. Behind them, a second Xan ship was engulfed by fire after the General had struck again.

Bastet suddenly leapt back, an enigmatic smile on her purple lips.

"Are you forfeiting?" Black Lys asked.

"Not at all!" replied the Immortal. "I merely herald your death," she added, pointing to a dot in the heavens.

Very quickly, the dot grew until it became the silhouette of a man dressed in a dark green suit, his chest adorned with the black scarab of Set. His face was covered with a golden mask, and Cendrine knew at once it was Amon, the one who had almost killed Ra in Boston. The green-garbed warrior sliced through the sky at high speed and landed right in front of Anhur, causing the ground beneath his feet to crack. Smaller than the General, Amon nevertheless exuded an aura of palpable power.

The Immortal made no mistake and carefully grasped his sword.

"Who are you?" he asked. "Another traitor?"

But Amon remained silent, motionless.

Anhur raised his weapon and struck with all his might. The blade touched the neck of the masked warrior and broke cleanly. Then Amon raised his fist and punched the General's jaw. The Immortal was sent sprawling several feet away, his face bleeding. Nevertheless, he got up and wiped his mouth. Amon took off, flying low, and hit his opponent with all the strength of his momentum. The two fighters broke through a building. Anhur, his two fists joined, hammered Amon. The two giants exchanged mighty blows, the echoes of which shattered all the window. But it quickly became obvious that the General was no match for the green-garbed warrior. He was strong, inhumanly so, but Amon was stronger—and more resilient.

Seeing the General in trouble, Black Lys wanted to rush to help him, but Bastet jumped in front of her.

"Now it's my turn to keep you busy, mortal bitch," purred the beautiful Immortal.

As the two women began to fight again, Anhur leapt back to gain some distance from his enemy. He brandished what was left of his sword, barely half a blade, and threw himself at his foe. With a skillful feint, he sliced around the silent warrior and quickly aimed for his face. But Amon did not dodge. The broken sword struck his golden mask—and shattered!

"By all the eggs of Etarr!" raged the General.

Amon tried to grab him, but Anhur quickly stepped back and got out of reach. He concentrated all his psychic power in his right hand and shaped it into a ball of coruscating energy. When Amon stepped forward, he threw it at him and a maelstrom of destruction soon engulfed the place where they stood. The building above collapsed entirely, and they became buried under an avalanche of stone blocks and metal beams. A cloud of dust spread throughout the neighborhood, blinding the other fighters and bringing a deadly silence.

Everyone held their breath as the dust slowly dissipated, leaving behind a spectacle of utter desolation. Where a tall tower had once proudly stood, now only scattered debris remained.

A pile of rocks suddenly shook and the shape of Amon painfully emerged, as he pushed aside the blocks of stone that had collapsed on him. His uniform was torn in several places and he was staggering. His half-exposed body bore the scars of Anhur's attack. Nevertheless, he appeared to have survived the blast. With one arm, he lifted the horribly bruised body of the General out of the rubble. Black Lys felt her throat contracting, but the Immortal was still alive—and kicking!

His two massive hands grabbed Amon's wrist in an attempt to get him to let go, but the Masked Warrior stood firm, clutching his opponent's neck, trying to strangle him.

Anhur, his legs dangling, kicked at the exact spot where his energy ball had hurt Amon. The other felt the blow. His grip loosened. He took a hesitant step backward. The General seized the opportunity to free himself and fell heavily to the ground. He was visibly at the end of his rope.

Amon remained a mystery. Even though his body was burned and bruised, his face, hidden behind the golden mask, was unreadable.

Anhur tried to get up, but his legs proved unable to support him. Amon grabbed him by the hair and held him up in front of him. Then, he violently punched the General in the stomach. The Immortal bent in half and fell to his knees.

Like a death machine, Amon raised his fist again. Anhur did not look away. He was a valiant soldier to the end; he looked at death straight in the eyes and defied it with a mirthless smile.

The masked warrior struck again and again, until the General finally collapsed, having breathed his last.

A cry of horror choked in Black Lys' throat as the sinister pounding of Amon's fists against the General's flesh filled her ears. Anger overwhelmed her and she attacked Bastet with all her might. Surprised by this outburst, the beautiful Immortal leapt backward and retreated.

The Hexagoneer took the opportunity to rush towards the General's body. Amon raised his head to the skies and took off, indifferent to all this, as if he had been summoned elsewhere. He was followed by Bastet, who also disappeared amongst the Xans.

Cendrine knelt beside Anhur and gently cradled his head. The Immortal tried to speak, but it was already too late. His vision became blurred, but he had time to smile one last time at the Frenchwoman before expiring.

Black Lys hugged her body. She didn't cry; she would only allow herself that luxury after the battle was over, after Anhur's assassins had been punished. She had not known the General for long, but she had fought by his side, and that was enough for her to take the measure of this extraordinary man, whose death was an immeasurable loss for Heliopolis.

Around her, the guards gathered to form a defensive circle. They confronted the Xans who, taking advantage of the death of their enemies' commanding officer, were intent on regaining the upper hand.

Finally, Black Lys stood up, taking a long breath. In her hands, the twin bio-electric blades screamed. And she leapt into the fray, leading the attack, determined to avenge Anhur's death at all costs.

Above Heliopolis, Ra slalomed between the cruisers. His mind probed each ship in search of Set's psychic signature. He knew that the battle in the streets below would not end until after he confronted his brother. Either he would convince him to put an end to this madness, or he would have to force him to do so...

Xan hovercrafts attacked him, but the Immortal easily repelled them. In cold anger, he unleashed his telekinetic powers and tore apart every vehicle that dared to assault him. His psionic force field deflected their laser fire and the aliens quickly realized they were helpless against this being with a golden aura that flew through the heavens. So they retreated to a higher altitude and dispatched a massive vessel to stop him. As Ra concentrated to prepare for battle, a flying platform detached itself from the side of the ship and floated directly toward him. On it was Set. He was a man of slender appearance, with a shaved head and a cruel look. He was dressed in a dark green outfit emblazoned with his emblem—the black scarab. At his side stood the ever-faithful Athor.

"My dear brother," said Set ironically, "I understand that you are looking for me?"

Ra chose to hover in front of the platform, facing the all-too-familiar silhouette of his brother—his enemy. The two Immortals gazed upon each other with contempt, resentment and hatred in. their eyes.

"Stop this madness immediately!" Ra ordered. "Your fight is with me—not with the rest of our kind! Or else, I'll be forced to destroy you."

"Oh, come on, do you really think you're in a position to give me orders? Or even negotiate? Open your eyes, Ra. Heliopolis burns at my feet!"

A powerful rage seized the mind of the rightful king of Heliopolis, but he controlled himself.

"Your madness has endured far too long," he spat. "How could you ally yourself with these alien mercenaries to bring death to your brothers. What happened to your honor?"

"My honor once commanded me to lead our people to greatness!" replied Set, his features distorted by contempt. "While you promised them nothing but endless stagnation, I offered them the world, but these fools turned me down and chased me away. They no longer deserved to partake in my glory! If in order to fulfill my destiny, I must level Heliopolis to its last stone, then so be it!"

Ra understood that he had truly lost his brother; his redemption was no longer possible: he had gone too far;

his madness consumed him and he was nothing but hatred towards all. He suddenly felt very tired and sad.

"Then I shall stop you, here and now," he replied. "Even if it means your death."

Ra unleashed his telekinetic power and released a psionic bolt that could have leveled a mountain, directing it right at Set and Athor. However, they remained unmoved. The golden ray passed through them, blurring their silhouettes for a second, before hitting the ship behind them. It triggered a series of explosions in the vessel which started to collapse upon itself. One louder detonation sent it crashing down into the towers of Heliopolis. But Set and Athor remained standing upon their aerial platform.

"I see!" said Set mockingly. "You thought we were really here. You're still so naive, brother! That's what's you will lose."

Ra remained still for a moment, then began to shake as a psychic scream exploded in his head. He saw painful images of Anhur confronting Amon and perishing under his blows... Head the death cry of the General... At once, he looked around and saw the golden masked warrior taking off and flying in the direction of the Arsenal.

Set's mental projection now smiled insanely.

"Ha! Your pathetic new allies won't be of any help to you. Anhur already fell; the others will soon follow. I will now join my champion to watch the final act of this play. Farewell, dear brother!"

The illusion vanished. Ra felt overwhelmed. He had just been tricked while one of his oldest friends had died in battle. His accursed brother had been playing him for a fool too long and his friends were paying the price. Despair threatened to overwhelm him, but he clung to the image of his comrades from Hexagon still fighting valiantly to defend his people. With fierce determination, he set out in pursuit of Amon.

Dominik Nero knew that his armor wouldn't last much longer. The stupendous amount of energy that ran through it, taken from Heliopolis' solar plant, was slowly but surely contributing to its destruction. Its internal circuitry was melting, the metal was overheating, the sensors were going haywire... He himself was being roasted... He had shot down ten of the Xan vessels, wiping out half of their strike force. He had seen more ships going down in flames and presumed it was Ra's handiwork. All in all, three-quarters of the alien fleet had been destroyed...

Alerts were flashing on his visor telling him that his armor was reaching the breaking point. Already, he couldn't move as he wanted; the electro-synaptic relays had been disabled...

"Sweet," called Dominik, "I need you to unplug everything; otherwise, I'm going to be toast—literally."

"*Yes, I see that*," replied his girlfriend. "*All sensors are in the red.*"

With a hissing sound, the power cables that connected the Dark Flyer to the solar pyramid disconnected. The energy level dropped drastically and Dominik felt the full weight of his suit suddenly falling on his body. He winced and opened the visor to get some fresh air. As a pleasant breeze caressed his face, he saw two ships pointing their guns at him.

"Oops," he muttered. "Bad timing."

Laser fire rained down on him. In a desultory gesture, he crossed his arms. A devastating explosion occurred only a few feet in front of him and he was thrown far back. He crashed against and through the wall of a building and landed in a vast library. A little bewildered, he straightened himself, resting on one elbow. Pieces of his armor were strewn all over the floor. He took off his helmet but kept the com, slipping an earpiece into his hear.

"Sweet, what happened?" he asked. "How come I'm still alive? What did you do?"

"*Dominik, are you all right?*" she replied, an edge of panic in her voice. "*I used a bio-dome to shield you— it's a force field intended to absorb lightning during a storm. I thought it might do the same with their lasers...*"

"And it did beautifully, my wonderful darling! You just saved my life!"

The Dark Flyer got up and got rid of the half-burned remains of his armor. His entire body was drenched with sweat.

"But now, I'm no good for much," he said with a note of regret.

He went down the building and out into the street. The neighborhood in which he had landed was still reasonably peaceful; the Xans were busy elsewhere. But he could still see the sinister silhouettes of their remaining ships in the sky above, as well as swarms of hovercrafts zipping about the city.

Several guards came to meet him. They, too, seemed had been severely tested and their features reflected the fatigue of the battle. Some were wounded.

"Are you all right?" asked an officer.

"I've been better, but I'm still alive," replied the Dark Flyer. "However, I have been stripped of my weapons..."

One of the guards handed him a crystalline tube, a kind of laser gun. Dominik took it with gratitude and set off with small squad towards the center of town. He could no longer count on his armor and he felt naked without it...

The Mysterious Archer had ran out of arrows and now fought hand-to-hand, his hexagonium tonfas mercilessly striking down all the Xans who dared to tackle him. At his side, Rakar fought in the same manner; his tomahawk and cutlass were covered with dark, alien blood. Thanks to Captain Sebek's time slowing power, they still had a small advantage, but their position had deteriorated since they had succeeded in taking control of the intersection.

The Xans had rushed *en masse* to overwhelm them and, even without the support of their tanks, their sheer numbers had forced the defenders to retreat step by step. The Immortals had fallen, one after the other, after a valiant fight. Now, only the two Hexagoneers and Sebek remained to block the avenue leading to the Arsenal.

Suddenly, a deafening explosion made them raise their eyes. In the sky above, Ra had just thrown himself at another flying warrior, whom the Archer recognized immediately: Amon!

The King of Heliopolis had intercepted his foe and struck him with all his telekinetic power. Surprised and visibly wounded, Amon lost altitude before recovering. The two superhumans began a complex aerial battle.

"We won't be able to hold this position for long!" Rakar shouted over the tumult. "We must reach Blackie Sullivan."

The Mysterious Archer nodded. Standing in the midst of a dozen Xan bodies, he felt each of his muscles screaming in pain; he was exhausted as never before.

"You're right. Let's fall back," he replied.

"You two go ahead and get your companion," Sebek shouted. "I'll hold them off here."

Rakar wanted to object, but the Archer nodded. He understood that the brave Captain would not yield and that it would be like an insult to stop him from engaging into this last fight. The Lakota shaman bit his lips before saluting the valiant Immortal.

"Good luck, Sebek!" he said. "We'll be back with reinforcements."

"It has been my honor to fight alongside Hexagon," replied the Captain.

Rakar and the Archer turned and ran toward the Arsenal. They never looked back. They knew that Sebek would give his life rather than let a single Xan go through.

"*Black Lys,*" called the Archer telepathically. "*We're abandoning our current position. We're going to the Arsenal to assist Fred. How are things on your end?*"

"*Anhur has fallen,*" replied Cendrine. "*We're still defending the palace. I can't join you; there are too many of them here...*"

The Archer sensed a flood of violent emotions—grief, rage, hatred. Suddenly, another voice broke in.

"*Cendrine, I'll be there in a minute with a platoon of guards,*" Dominik said. "*I lost my armor, but I can still be useful on their Atum computer, like Sweet. We...*"

The telepathic communication was interrupted. They heard a great crash. Ra and Amon, embraced in a mortal combat, had just hit the roof of the Arsenal.

Rakar and the Archer looked at each other and quickened their pace.

Inside the Arsenal, Blackie Sullivan was furious at having to wait alone in what he thought was basically a creepy warehouse. He was sure that his powers would be far more useful on the battlefield. He had proved it in New York. He could shoot down an alien vessel with his bare hands! But he also understood what was at stake and didn't want to disappoint the Black Lys. So he had waited.

At first, he had hoped that some Xans would reach him, but in vain. Then he remembered that the Mysterious Archer and Rakar were tasked with holding them back. He knew that these two could stop even a well-armed alien army...

Though their telepathic channel, he learned of Anhur's death. This only increased his anger because he had liked the bombastic General and would have preferred to fight by his side. He felt Cendrine's sorrow, Ra's despair, the Dark Flyer's helplessness and the Archer and Rakar's sense of resignation... The battle wasn't going well...

Then, he heard the crashing sound above his head.

Blackie Sullivan got up from the chair where he had been sitting. At last, some action! The ceiling above his head shattered and two silhouettes crashed to the ground: Ra, whose swollen face was already proof of the power of his opponent, and Amon, the mysterious superhuman who served Set and whose strength equaled his own.

The master of dark matter smiled—an ugly smile that his old enemy Max Tornado would have immediately recognized. That was the smile of the old Blackie Sullivan. He knew he could unleash his powers without any need for restraint—both that of the mysterious Soul of Levan and those granted by the Fomore device on Mars. His body became surrounded by an aura of darkness, the dark energy lying in the folds of the universe, now crackling with rage...

Ahead of him, Amon, whose uniform was in tatters and whose torso bore an ugly burn, got up from amongst the debris. He was perfectly silent; his golden mask turned towards this new foe who was moving towards him. He took a step forward...

Elsewhere in the Arsenal, the Negatives sprang to life. Their massive granite silhouettes rose against this hostile intruder; a pulsating radiance surrounded them.

Fred decided to stand still and observe what was about to happen.

"You who do not belong in this sacred place, leave at once or suffer the consequences!" threatened one of the statues.

Amon didn't answer.

A Negative stepped towards him and the ground shook under his feet.

Only then did the silent warrior act. He grabbed the stone arm outstretched towards him and effortlessly lifted the statue off the ground. He then threw it at another Negative. The two sentinels collided violently and shattered into multiple pieces. Amon then grabbed the head of a third sentinel and tore it off in a prodigious display of strength. The beheaded Negative took one step forward then collapsed. The last remaining living statue clutched Amon in its mineral grip, but the masked warrior did not budge. Stretching out his muscles, he forced open the hand that held him, then struck the Negative on his chest, making him fall to the ground. He then took off and fell back upon the sentinel like a missile. The living statue exploded on impact. In less than five minutes, Amon had destroyed the powerful robots created by Ra.

The fight he had just witnessed only inspired Blackie Sullivan with the desire to fight this prodigious warrior. Fred noted that the Negatives had not neutralized Amon's powers, so that meant that he was not an Immortal, but something else. What that was mattered little to him, so eager he was to fight.

Suddenly, something entirely unexpected happened. Blackie Sullivan felt all his control of dark matter flowing away from him—inexplicably. In the space of a mere second, the Hexagoneer felt drained; he had just lost his most fearsome power!

"What the...?" he exclaimed, unable to explain what had happened.

Immediately, Amon rushed at him and punched him hard in the face. Blackie Sullivan was thrown against a shelf covered with strange weapons. He staggered back to his feet, half stunned. Few enemies had ever been capable of handling him like this—Max Tornado, his late brother Jeff...

"Now that only makes it more interesting," he muttered with a bloody smile.

And he threw himself at this masked opponent, hitting him with all his might.

Amon took the punch, but stepped back. Blackie made the most of his advantage. He threw a series of punches without giving his foe time to recover.

With no other way out, Amon took off and hovered in mid-air above his opponent in order to catch his breath. Then he fell right on top of him, but Blackie Sullivan had anticipated the move and only punched harder at the incoming warrior.

The two superhumans engaged in a struggle of pure strength, each trying to strike the other down, but they seemed too evenly matched for one to gain superiority over the other.

Fred stared at the golden mask and suddenly felt a strange sense of familiarity, as if he had faced Amon before. For a troubled moment, he took a step back, but his silent foe seized that opportunity, grabbing him by the arm and tackling him down to the ground. Ever resourceful, Blackie used this position to wrap his legs around Amon's neck. But the golden-masked warrior summoned all his strength and succeeded in lifting the Hexagoneer off the floor. He then slammed him against a wall before dropping him to the ground.

Blackie Sullivan felt pain in every inch of his body, but the joy the former astronaut took in the fight made him forget it. With a mighty kick, he swept Amon off his feet and, without giving his adversary time to pull himself back together, he grabbed his ankle and threw him against the shelves. Then he sprang back to his feet and pinned the masked warrior to the ground and began to hammer him with his fists.

Even without dark matter, I am still the strongest! he thought.

The power he had acquired when he and Max Worth had been caught in the explosion of that ancient Fomore machine on Mars had never failed him.

But Amon withstood his assault without registering any distress.

Suddenly, a thin crack appeared in his golden mask and widened almost imperceptibly.

Immediately, Blackie Sullivan stopped, his fists still in the air. A strange connection seemed to be taking shape—much to his surprise—between him and his opponent. Once more, he felt that sense of unexplainable familiarity... Then everything grew blurry and he passed out...

When he opened his eyes again, he saw not one but a dozen Amons surrounding him. He swiftly got back to his feet, ready to face these masked warriors. They rushed at him and rained blows of seismic force upon him. The only thing he could do was to fold his arms in front of his face to protect himself. Out of the corner of his eye, he saw Ra, standing on one elbow, blood flowing from his mouth, who shouted:

"Fred! It's just an illusion! Don't trust your eyes! It's only..."

Suddenly, Ben Leonard took his head in his hands and screamed in pain.

"Hush, brother," said a cruel voice, "you're going to spoil his surprise."

At once, Blackie Sullivan was able to perceive the shape of a man through the illusions that assailed him— a bald man with an evil face, who stood next to Ra— Set—and, a few steps away, an old man who was staring at him intensely, Athor—he who was called Master of Illusions...

Blackie Sullivan received another blow and that shock was enough to dispel the visions that tormented him. He could now clearly see Set keeping his brother at bay, using a painful mind-lock, while the old man had just pulled out a golden disk from a pile of weapons.

"Master, I've located the medallion," said Athor.

"Very good," Set rejoiced. "I can start the final phase of my plan."

Blackie took a few wobbly steps towards the two villains. His vision was still blurry and the sounds he heard only reached him muffled.

Set looked at him with something like grudging admiration.

"What stamina! What perseverance! It is a shame to have to..." but he quickly changed his mind and ordered: "But, no. No more delays. Amon, finish him off!"

A new avalanche of blows then fell on Blackie Sullivan; the warrior in the golden mask struck him tirelessly and repeatedly... Even a superhuman as powerful as the Fred Sullivan could no longer stand against such a mighty assault. He collapsed and sank into unconsciousness despite all his efforts.

The last image he saw was that of Set, Athor and Amon dematerializing, the silent warrior carrying Ra, unconscious, in his arms...

When Rakar and the Mysterious Archer finally reached the Arsenal, they found a stunned Blackie Sullivan and the scattered remains of the Negatives.

CHAPTER XI
Amon's Secret

The first thing Ra felt when he woke up was an intense pain in his head, like a high-pitched scream piercing his brain. Then he realized that that scream was, in fact, his own, a half-muffled groan that to his bruised senses sounded like an unbearable, strident shout.

He opened his eyes and found that he was in a room with bare walls, a door and no windows. A few steps away, he saw the sturdy figure of Amon just standing there, his arms folded. His uniform was new and he no longer bore the traces of the recent combat. His face remained hidden behind his feature-less golden mask.

When he tried to get up to face his foe, Ra discovered not only that his whole body was painful but that he was also tied up in some kind of metal throne. His wrists and ankles were shackled with thick iron bracelets. He could barely move. Despite the pain in his head, he focused his mental powers to try to destroy his chains, but to no avail. His telekinesis couldn't find any hold on them; not only the throne but also the walls, the door and the ceiling of the room remained unaffected. Obviously, Set had left nothing to chance. Everything here was immune to his powers. He tried to use Ra telepathy to probe this new environment but found that he could hardly reach beyond the room. He was truly isolated from the outside world and could not contact his allies.

The Immortal was not altogether surprised to still be alive. His brother was unable to kill him without first bragging about his plans and making him suffer first by displaying the extent of his triumph. It was not the first time he had ended up in Set's hands and he had always been able to turn the tables by taking advantage of this weakness. One would have thought that Set might have learned from his past mistakes but clearly, his megalomania was pathological.

Ra turned his eyes towards Amon. The mute warrior stood totally still. In fact, Ben could barely detect his breathing. He was like a statue, watching over his prisoner with robotic efficiency. Yet, something had changed since their first encounter in Boston... Ra felt it. The vast emptiness he had felt when he had first probed the warrior's mind had been replaced by a faint stirring. It was almost nothing, less than a murmur, but perhaps it was a path to understanding who Amon was, and how he could defeat him.

Ben Leonard examined his jailer with renewed scrutiny, looking for even the tiniest detail that might explain the change he had detected. And he found it! The golden mask, once immaculate, was now cracked. And it was from that tiny, almost undetectable fissure that the murmur he had sensed emanated. Emanated.

Exposing Amon's secret might be the weapon he needed to defeat Set. Ra took a deep breath and closed his eyes. He ignored his pain, relegating it to a corner of his mind, controlled his breathing and marshaled his mental powers. Then he sent a focused probe towards Amon. It found the crack and infiltrated it.

At first, Ra found only endless nothingness, like before. But as his probe dug even deeper, he began to see a faint glow in the darkness. He strengthened it, extended it, delving deeper into spiritual space, a plane where souls came into direct contact with one another. Slowly and methodically, he progressed with the patience of a surgeon.

The task was difficult. Ra was not an experienced telepath, like Set who could control entire populations with his mind. He was still new at this, but right now, it was his only weapon. He finally reached that minuscule light that pulsed faintly in the space where Amon's mind should have been. Ra then understood that the golden mask was itself a prison, a powerful psychic cage intended to cast the soul of its wearer into oblivion.

Ben immediately thought that if, somehow, he could free whoever Amon, truly was, then perhaps the mighty warrior would be grateful and would help them defeat Set.

The Immortal then proceeded to make contact with this enslaved mind. He went about it meticulously, searching for psychic fractures, circumventing psionic walls, avoiding all kinds of mental traps... It was a long and painstakingly difficult task. He couldn't tell if he had been at it for five hours or five years, but finally, he managed to knock down the last defense and reach the light within.

And there, he made a discovery that shook his very soul...

Amon was none other than Jeff Sullivan!
The *late* Jeff Sullivan!

Several months ago...

Jeff Sullivan woke up with a start, as if he had just had a particularly bad dream. He jumped to his feet thought he had somehow managed to escape from the clutches of the Necromancer (although he didn't remember how) and was ready to help his fellow Hexagoneers fight their arch-enemy.

More memories came rushing in... He had been captured by the diabolical madman... Taken to the villain's secret base on the Moon... Then, there had been a mighty explosion... And that's all he remembered![9]

Looking around him, he recognized a familiar landscape: New York. Had he been sent back to Earth? What about Hexagon and the Necromancer?

Jeff took a few steps through the streets of the city. His gold uniform was badly shredded, but it was no time to think about appearances. Something was wrong here, but what? He found himself in what looked like a slum: rundown buildings, a garbage-filled wasteland. In the distance, he could see the skyscrapers of New York... Suddenly, he stopped. He had just noticed many little silhouettes flying through the sky and around the buildings... Men... Women...

He looked around again and, this time, noticed the minute differences: a tag for a sports team that he didn't recognize, a half-destroyed billboard for a drink that didn't exist on *his* Earth...

The Man of Brass now understood his predicament. He was no longer on his world, but on another. This had happened to him once before, when he had inherited the Soul of Levan, the power of the Sullivans... In the event of his sudden death, his soul would transmigrate into a parallel Earth and reincarnate inside a body similar to his—another Jeff Sullivan!

Jeff's face broke into a gloomy smile. The fact that he was here meant that he had died on the Moon. But he had managed to return to his own world once before, after being thrown on an Earth where the Axis had won

---

[9] For more on this sequence of events, see *Strangers #1: Strangers in a Strange Land.*

World War II and the United States were living under Japanese occupation. He was confident that he could do the same again.

Suddenly, he heard the characteristic sounds of guns being fired. His training kicked in and he ran toward the noises. He came out onto an avenue encumbered with car wrecks and saw several scruffy men running away from a squadron of uniformed flying soldiers shooting at them. The weapons looked more sophisticated than what he was familiar with, and the uniforms, which included rounded helmets, dark goggles leather boots and belts, had a distinctive military look. He briefly wondered if he wasn't back on "Nazi-Earth" and these were not SS... But what surprised him the most was that these flying men were not wearing any jetpacks or anti-gravity devices. They were just... flying... levitating... under their own power.

Jeff experienced a moment's hesitation, but then decided to side with the fleeing civilians who were unarmed and running for their lives. Even if they were criminals, they surely didn't deserve to be shot like rabbits!

The Man of Brass took to the air and threw himself in front of the soldiers The men hesitated for a moment, then fired at this new target. The projectiles hit Jeff but just bounced off him. He grabbed the rifle of one of the soldiers who stood in his path and crushed it as if it were made of plastic, then threw it at another soldier. Acting with lightning speed, he grabbed two other men and smashed their heads into each other. Behind him, another soldier suddenly pulled out a different, heavier type of weapon and shot it at Jeff. A translucent material spurted out of it, forming a bubble around the hero, imprisoning him. However, Jeff felt the material hardening with his fingertips and, as the uniformed men were surrounding him, struck it with all his might. The polymer shattered and he was free again.

This time, the soldiers looked at him, then at each other, then fled, flying away as fast as they could.

The Man of Brass landed in front of the civilians who had witnessed the battle with a mixture of amazement and suspicion. They were exchanging frantic murmurs and looked as afraid of him as the soldiers had been. Jeff spread his hands apart as a sign of peace, to show that he had no hostile intentions.

"Don't be afraid," he said. "My name is Jeff Sullivan. I'm not from around here. Maybe you could help me find my way home?"

The men stared at him but still looked as if they didn't trust him. Then Jeff noticed something very strange: everyone's eyes were different. They had no eyelids and their pupils and the irises were combined into a single black circle. It gave them an unblinking, staring look that was closer to that of a bug than a human.

"He's a Flyer," said one man. "He can't be trusted."

"But he saved us," protested another.

"It could be a trick," said a third.

Jeff sensed their hostility. Now, they were no longer frightened, but were threatening with makeshift weapons: a rock, a lead pipe... He knew he had nothing to fear but wanted desperately to avoid another confrontation.

"Everybody stop!" shouted a voice coming from an alley.

A young black man with a shaved head and dressed in a patchwork of unmatched clothes had just stepped out. The other men parted to let him through.

"Look at him," continued the newcomer. "Do you see his eyes... and the strength he displayed in chasing the Flyers away... He's not one of them; he's telling the truth; he's a stranger here."

Jeff, relieved, held his hand out to the young man who shook it.

"I'm Marik," he said.

"And I'm Jeff Sullivan."

"Thank you for what you did earlier, Jef Sulvan. But why did you take sides?"

Jeff shrugged.

"Well, it all didn't seem very fair to me," he replied. "These armed men against unarmed civilians... On my world—which we call Earth—I protect those who can't defend themselves."

Marik looked at him with his dark, unblinking eyes and nodded.

"Our world—Erden—could use someone like you. Do you feel like helping us out?"

"Marik, don't you think that..." interrupted one of the civilians.

"Shut up!" spat out the young man. "Don't you forget who you're talking to."

The man who had spoken stepped back and lowered his head. Jeff hesitated, not knowing what to answer.

"This is not my world. Do I have the right to interfere? I really only want to go home."

"I get it," said Marik. "I'll make you a deal: help us out and we'll find a way to send you back to that... Earth."

"I can't promise you anything until I know more about the situation here."

Marik bit his lips, thinking about the best way to convince this champion to side with them.

"OK, I'll take you to someone who can explain the situation on Erden much better than I could."

He took a scarf out of his pocket. Jeff raised an eyebrow. But if that was his only option...

He agreed to let himself be blindfolded. Then he was led through a maze of alleys and buildings, until he could no longer tell where he was.

In the present time, Ra reluctantly pulled himself out of Jeff Sullivan's memories which he had been watching unfold. He felt frustrated because he hadn't yet learned how Jeff had become Set's slave. As one might do with a film, he speeded up the deciphering of his memories, while allowed himself a few stops to better grasp the sequence of events.

The Man of Brass had been led into a secret lair of the Resistance, located deep inside the sewers of Megapol—that was the name of the city where he had arrived, the capital of the Transamerican Confederation. There, Marik had introduced him to a woman named Eva, with a thin white scar on her face that barely impacted her savage beauty.

Jeff and Eva spent a long time chatting about the history of this strange world in which he had arrived. On this parallel Earth the natives called Erden, history had followed a path similar to that which Jeff knew, until 1795 when a strange meteorite had fallen in Yorkshire. For reasons as yet unclear, it had induced a mutation in the human genome—but not in everyone, only in some. Some persons were henceforth born with the ability to defy gravity. The distribution of the mutation appeared to be totally random, ignoring distinctions of class, sex or race, but was transmissible from one generation to another.

It took just about a century for human societies, all over the globe, to fracture into two castes: that of those who could take to the air, known unimaginatively as "Flyers," and those who remained hopelessly earth-bound, who became derisively known as "Crawlers."

Another century passed during which the Flyers gained the upper hand and became the elite of humanity, seizing the reins of power everywhere. In all nations, an ugly form of segregation evolved in which the Crawlers were relegated to the lower rungs of society, condemned to the dirtiest, lowest and less paid jobs. By the time the 20th century reached its end, the Crawlers everywhere were sub-citizens deprived of many human rights.

Then, at the dawn of this new century, a resistance movement had sprung up, here and there but especially in the Transamerican Confederation where the values enshrined by its Founders remained strong. Rebels organized themselves, all over the world, came into contact with each other, gained strength... Demonstrations took place, but they only led to bloody repression.

Despite it all, however, attitudes were changing. The Flyers were no longer a monolithic block. Some privileged people sided with the Crawlers, and minority political parties campaigned for the abolition of segregation. A few smaller Regions even passed laws to abolish segregation...

The xenophobia that was deeply ingrained in the minds of the Flyers of Erden, however, was given a boost by the appearance on September 11, 2001, of two men, extradimensional travelers from another world. They were Jean Vlad and the strange being known only as The Other.[10] Their visit on Erden was brief, but its revelation of the existence of other worlds shook its beliefs to its very foundations. In response to what became known as the "attacks" of September 11, Erden moved towards closer unity between its various Federations, moved by a new charismatic leader called Wrack.

The détente that had sprung between Flyers and Crawlers became a thing of the past. Finding inspiration in Wrack's racist message, the Flyers reverted to the old policies of oppression and segregation. In response, the Resistance became more radical and started to resort to terrorism as its most common means of action. An infernal cycle of violence, persecution and reprisals, had begun...

Eva could not promise that she would be able to help Jeff Sullivan go home, but she knew that under Senator Gruul of Megapol, the Transamerican scientists had already begin to work on finding ways to travel between worlds—and a few of them were secretly sympathetic to the Resistance's goals. She hoped that soon, they might find a way to assist the Man of Brass in his desire to return to Earth. In the meantime, she assured him that if he helped the Resistance, he would change the lives of countless people for the better. Jeff gave in.

The months that followed were a series of clashes, both physical and symbolic. "Jef Sulvan," as he became known, was the only superhuman on Erden. Not only could he fly, but he had Herculean strength and was almost indestructible. The Resistance began to score

---

[10] The full story of Jean Vlad and the Other's visit to Erden will be told in a future volume of *Wampus*.

points against the fascist hordes and the movement began to spread.

The Man of Brass became a symbol—the promise of a better world for people who had never dared to look up at the sky. In order to hide the fact that he came from another world, that would only have triggered more xenophobia, Eva had had the idea of making Jeff wear dark goggles that obscured his "repulsive, glaucous orbs" as someone had once called his eyes.

More than once, Jeff questioned his right to intervene in the history of a world that was not his own. This dilemma sometimes kept him up at night. He wondered how long it would be until he would be able to go home, to see his wife Mary and his daughter Kathryn...

And then one day, after more than a year of combat, the moment came...

Ra paused again. He smiled. He had not had the opportunity to know Jeff Sullivan, having joined Hexagon after his presumed death, but he recognized in what he saw the man that everyone had described to him. A true hero not so much because of his powers but because of the greatness of his spirit.

The Man of Brass still fought for justice even on Erden, a world so far from his own, despite his own doubts and crushing loneliness.

The Immortal's anger grew at the thought that his perfidious brother Set had reduced this extraordinary man to a mere killing machine. It was time to find out how that had happened...

True to her word, Eva told Jeff about a secret site located in the Nevada desert. According to her informers, this was where the most secret research into transdimensional travel was being conducted. The Man of Brass had fought long and loyally for the Resistance and deserved a chance to go home—if he could.

Before he left, Jeff gave Eva a last piece of advice that he had kept for himself until now, being reluctant to draw other members of his extradimensional family into the conflict.

"If I don't come back," he said, "which truthfully, I hope, seek my brother Doug. Once I have left Erden, he will be this world's legitimate heir to my powers. If he is like his counterpart on my world, he will be a good man, one whom you can rely on to become your new champion."

"Dug Sulvan... I understand..." replied Eva.

Jeff Sullivan was now walking across the Nevada desert. He did not use his powers and wore the black goggles that hid his true origins. With his ten-day beard and dusty clothes, he didn't look much like the hero that all the Crawlers were cheering for, and it suited him just fine.

He walked towards the coordinates of the secret base that Eva had given him—it was called "Area 105." He chuckled at the thought that Erden's Transamerica had obviously more secret bases than his own U.S. of A. He was trying to not get his hopes too high by not thinking about his wife, his daughter and his teammates from Hexagon. In a way, he had really died on the Moon in the battle against the Necromancer. He was certainly dead in the eyes of his loved ones. Maybe Doug suspected he wasn't really gone, but his return would surely be a shock to the others...

When he saw the Area 105 base in the middle of the desert, Jeff at first thought it was a mirage. A persistent wind was stirring up dust devils between rows of hangar-like, windowless buildings. A large sign on the road indicated that this was a property of the Transamerican Government and required visitors to turn back under pain of various penalties.

As he got closer, Jeff noticed something unusual. Behind one of the hangars was a saucer-shaped vehicle, surrounded by strange, faceless beings. They were busy loading various equipment obviously taken from the base into the saucer. Their featureless bodies, smooth faces and mechanical gestures indicated they were androids of some kind. The fact that the ground was littered with the dead bodies of soldiers was further proof that this was not a peaceful operation but a heist.

Suddenly, two men emerged from the belly of the spacecraft: one was an old man with a long, braided beard wearing an anachronistic toga; the second was a bald man dressed in a green uniform with a black scarab. They watched the progress of the work.

Jeff decided to get closer to hear what they were saying.

"This man Wrack was telling the truth, Master," said the old man. "These people are working on transdimensional travel."

"But they have not perfected it yet, Athor," replied the bald man. "For my plan to succeed, I will need more advanced technology."

"Still, what we took here," said Athor, pointing at the equipment being transported into the saucer-shaped craft by the faceless androids, "will prove useful."

"That, it will indeed, and..." Suddenly, he stopped in mid-sentence and turned around.

Jeff knew at once that the bald man had become aware of his presence, although he didn't know how. Maybe the alien—for that was what he was, surely—was endowed with psychic powers?

Jeff noticed that his eyes and those of the old man called Athor were similar to those of the humans of Earth. His heart beat a little faster. Maybe these two came from his own world?

"We must leave no witnesses behind!" said the bald man. "Faceless Ones! Eliminate this intruder!"

The androids stopped what they were doing and turned toward Jeff. They stretched out their hands and rays burst forth from their fingers, bathing Jeff in a shower of deadly energy. The blast would have disintegrated anyone else, but he was the Man of Brass!

Jeff felt anger burning within him. He had fought to bring peace to Erden, combating its xenophobic prejudices, and now two hostile invaders seemingly from Earth had attacked it, slaughtered its soldiers and were engaged in stealing its research in the very technology he needed to go home!

He took off and the shock wave carved a crater beneath his feet. He zoomed towards the Faceless Ones and hit them hard. Some were thrown against the saucer while others crashed into the buildings. Jeff kept hammering them with all his strength, smashing them to pieces which scattered them around him. The energy bolts they fired at him caused him pain but did not hurt him.

In a matter of minutes, the Man of Brass had gotten rid of them and, barely out of breath, turned his attention towards the bald man and the old man.

167

"Fascinating!" said the former.

"This may be just what you sought, O Master Set," said Athor. "A champion powerful enough to defeat even the accursed Ra!"

"Yes, faithful Athor. I believe that you are right," replied Set.

He then directed his gaze at Jeff and the Man of Brass suddenly felt his mind being pierced by fiery daggers. He grabbed his head in his hands and gaped in a silent scream. All the dark feelings he had ever felt since his arrival on Erden—loneliness, guilt, doubt, despair, anger—tuned against him like hungry ghosts and assailed him from within. He knew that he was being psychically attacked by this man named Set but was powerless to stop it. His powers were in the domain of the physical, not the mental.

Despite the pain, he managed to take a step forward, flexing his muscles, but suddenly, all the sand and dust around him rose up in a whirlwind and blocked his view.

When that phenomenon subsided, Jeff found himself once more surrounded by the Faceless Ones who threw themselves at him. He defended himself, striking down as many of them as he could, despite being burned by their energy bolts, but meanwhile, the pain in his skull kept getting worse. Then, when he was sufficiently weakened, a commanding voice told him to give up the fight and sleep... sleep...

Jeff went down hard. He could no longer think coherently and felt nothing but pain. He tried one last time to get up but failed. Then an immense darkness filled his mind and he passed out.

Ra had suffered watching the doomed plight of the Man of Brass. He knew better than anyone the extent of Set's mental powers and Athor's deadly illusions. Jeff Sullivan had not been able to resist either, and that's how the evil Immortal had managed to capture him.

Ra could easily guess the rest. Set had taken Jeff back to one of the Mirrorverses in which he dwelt and used that fiendish gold mask to brainwash him and keep his under his control. Now, he had a champion more powerful than even the Immortals—Earth's greatest hero!

Later, he had somehow learned on Zhud's far more advanced transdimendional technology, managed to track down one of Melanos' abandoned bases, and there, found what he needed to prepare the invasion of Heliopolis.

It had been Set's little joke to name his new servant "Amon" after their long-gone brother, and with Jeff's power at his command, he had been able to destroy the Negatives and even defeat Blackie Sullivan by reclaiming the power of the Soul of Levan. Reduced to the state of a soulless puppet, the Man of Brass had fought at the height of his power, being impervious to pain, fear and doubt. He was the perfect weapon...

Ben Leonard severed the telepathic link and returned to his body. He opened his eyes and smiled. Before withdrawing from Jeff's mind, he had focused on the crack in the Golden Mask and planted a psychic seed that he hoped would germinate when the so-called Amon would be fighting again.

Set had made a mistake, one that many others had made before him: he had underestimated the power and resilience of Hexagon. Ra knew without a doubt that his teammates would soon come to his rescue.

Then, exhausted by his long psychic journey, he, too, sank into unconsciousness, but with this comforting thought in mind.

On Erden, this second, and definitely hostile, incursion by extradimensional visitors, only boosted Wrack's political aspirations—as he had intended by providing Set with information in the first place. He succeeded in unifying the planet under his banner, becoming Supreme Commander Wrack, and then turned his attention to other worlds.

Since the best form of defense was attack, under his leadership, Eden started preparing for war—a war of conquest, aimed at other Earths.

But the Resistance had not remained idle. Eva remembered Jeff's advice, and with Malik's help, they finally located Jeff's Erden-born brother—Dug Sulvan—and his Erden-born daughter, Katrix.

Once in possession of their powers, it would be they who would lead the Resistance...[11]

---

[11] The story of Dug and Katrix Sulvan and the Resistance on Erden will be told in a forthcoming episode of *Strangers*.

CHAPTER XII
Riposte

The siege of Heliopolis had ended as abruptly as it had begun. While the fighting was still raging in front of the palace and in some neighborhoods, everything had come to a stop.

Despite having lost fifteen ships, the Xans were still gaining ground but suddenly, they had withdrawn and returned to their crafts, which had then left through the tear in the sky. The gap had closed again, and it was as if it had never opened.

While the guards around the Black Lys rejoiced at this apparent retreat of their opponents, the swordswoman felt as if they had just been defeated. It was undeniable that the aliens had had the upper hand, so why had hey left? The answer was obvious and unavoidable: they had done so because Set had succeeded in getting his hands on what he had been looking for... Maybe he had never intended to conquer the city, after all... But then, what *was* his objective?

As the Immortals organized themselves to help the wounded and repair their city, the Black Lys walked towards the Arsenal, feeling only weariness and mourning the loss of General Anhur.

On the way, she met the Dark Flyer, trudging along accompanied by a few guards. Dominik Nero was in a pitiful state: his skin was burned in many places and his face reflected his immense fatigue.

"Cendrine, what's going on?" he asked, as troubled as she was by the apparent retreat of Set's troops.

"I don't know, but I fear the worst. We must get to the Arsenal *très vite*."

Dominik nodded and followed her.

As they arrived in sight of the imposing greyish bunker, they came upon Rakar and the Mysterious Archer. The area was still littered with smoking carcasses and Xan corpses.

"I see that you two had a good time," said Dominik making his way through the chaos.

"From what I saw down here, you didn't do too badly either up there," complimented Rakar.

"Yeah, but my armor is toast."

A movement from somewhere in the pile of bodies suddenly caught their attention. Lying on the ground, Captain Sebek was struggling to stay conscious. Wounded everywhere, covered in blood, he refused the embrace of death.

Cendrine leaned over him and straightened him but gave her teammates a concerned look.

"Sweet honey?" called Dominik on the intercom.

"*I'm right here.*"

"Send a medvac to my position ASAP."

"*Ten-Four,*" replied the young woman. "*I'm dispatching Immortals with healing powers. One will be with you in less than five minutes.*"

Indeed, three minutes later, a female Immortal with a thin face and long, frayed ivory toga came gliding through the air and landed near them.

She immediately knelt beside Sebek and brushed his body with the palms of her hands. A blue radiance bathed the body of the captain, whose suffering features were finally soothed. His breathing also returned to a regular rhythm.

The Immortal then noticed the wounds of the Hexagoneers: the Black Lys' various cuts and gashes, the Dark Flyer's burns, etc., and cured them in the same manner.

"Wow! That is a damn effective treatment!" enthused Dominik. "Thank you, er, Miss...?"

"My name is Isis," replied the healer, introducing herself. "Sebek is my brother, and I thank you for looking after him until I arrived."

Suddenly, a badly beaten Blackie Sullivan appeared, limping. Even Cendrine was surprised. That someone was able to beat the master of dark matter so thoroughly...

"Isis, I'm afraid we still need your skills," said the beautiful swordswoman.

The immortal nodded and bathed the newcomer with her regenerative energy.

Blackie fell heavily to the ground and sat there, immersed in his thoughts. Even though Isis had healed his wounds, his pride was hurt. But, above all, many questions swirled in his head, unanswered.

"Fred, what happened in there?" asked the Black Lys pointing at the Arsenal.

"Ra and Amon crashed into the building. Then Set and the old guy showed up. I tried to stop them but they sicced Amon on me. We fought; I lost. My guess is, whatever Set came looking for, he found it."

"Which would explain the Xan withdrawal," noted the Archer.

"This guy Amon," continued Fred, "he smashed up the Negatives like they were toys. Also, he took my powers... The powers I acquired when I inherited the Soul of Levan... They just evaporated, like that!" He snapped his fingers. "Fighting him was really weird, like

I knew him... After that, Set and the old guy left with some kind of sun disk... and they took Ra with them."

Blackie Sullivan held out his hand and concentrated. Suddenly, a tiny spot of black light appeared, creating a minute gravitational singularity. He closed his fist and made it disappear.

"Weird. My control over dark matter seems to have returned," he said.

"This Amon may possess the ability to negate his opponent's powers?" suggested Rakar.

"No. If so, I would have lost my strength too," said Fred. "But it only affected the Soul of Levan. I felt it fade inside me as I approached him."

A silence greeted this observation. As if their enemy was not powerful enough, now he seemed capable of affecting the strongest of them.

"Let's not overthink it," said the Mysterious Archer. "Let's return at the palace and talk to Osir."

Cendrine nodded. They had too many questions; it was time to find the answers.

Osir became very upset when Blackie Sullivan described the artifact that Set had stolen from the Arsenal. He paced back and forth in a briefing room set up inside the Palace of Heliopolis. Standing around a polished marble table, the Hexagoneers threw a glance at Captain Sebek who had insisted on taking part in the meeting against his sister's advice. His face was equally gloomy.

"Dare I say, you obviously know what this is all about," said Lys.

Osir finally stopped pacing and sat heavily into a chair.

"Alas, er do," replied the Regent. "What you described I called the Sacred Medallion of Ra. It is an object of immense power. Our king used to wear it, but as evil Ser tried to steal it, he finally decided to leave it under lock and key in the Arsenal."

"Looks like Set's efforts finally paid off," Dominik said, with more than a hint of irony.

Black Lys threw a disapproving glance at him and encouraged Osir to continue.

"What it really is, is an energy source," the Regent explained. "Our science captured the power of a star in this simple medallion... A feat that has never been repeated since..."

"So this tiny disk contains the power of the sun," said Blackie Sullivan, who, as a former astronaut, was immediately impressed. "For anyone who could harness such a reserve of energy, nothing would be impossible."

"The Gateway of the Gods... the Medallion of Ra... I'm a little lost here," said Rakar. "What is Set trying to accomplish if he wasn't trying to conquer Heliopolis?"

"Jukka, do you have an idea?" Cendrine asked.

The Mysterious Archer took his time answering.

"I'm sorry, this time, even I am having trouble seeing the big picture. I see the overall picture, but I'm missing a piece—an essential piece—to put it all together."

"Set used the Gateway to come here and steal that Medallion," said the Dark Flyer. "Perhaps he just intends to use it as a kind of doomsday device to blackmail all of Earth into surrendering to his rule?"

"But why the Medallion?" said Sebek. "There are other weapons in that Arsenal that are mightier, deadlier, and easier to use."

"This is frustrating," raged the Black Lys. "We don't know our opponent, we don't know his plan, and we don't even know where he is! And to top it all, he's taken one of ours…"

Everyone in the room knew how much Set hated his brother, so no one dared voice their concerns aloud. After all, the evil Immortal had murdered Ra once already!

"We're wasting our time," said Fred Sullivan. What we should concentrate on is finding Set and stopping him at all costs. Everything else is a distraction."

Cendrine smiled in spite of herself. Blackie was a pragmatic man without many scruples, but this time, she had to admit that he was not wrong. She looked around the table, but the other Hexagoneers just shrugged without offering any other proposals.

"So finding Set is our #1 priority," said Dominik "But for all we know, he could be in another dimension or anywhere else in our universe thanks to the tech he stole."

"But any tech leaves a signature behind," said Rakar. "Can we track it?"

"We know it comes from Zhud, and we've had past experience with Zhuvian technology," added the Archer, pensive.

A silence fell in the room.

"I bet your girlfriend can do it!" said Blackie Sullivan. "I haven't been with you long, but I noticed, she's always the one who comes up with idea in situations like these."

"Let's ask her," said the Dark Flyer.

He put his hand to his ear, where the intercom was located and called.

"Honey, can you hear me?"

"*Let me guess: you guys need me again?*" answered the young prodigy in a sarcastic tone.

"Well, er, yes," said Dominik, a little sheepishly. "Set took Ben and some kind of doomsday device and scampered away... We need some way of finding out where he's gone asap... You see, he's been using the tech he stole from Melanos, and we thought..."

"That, I can do. Easy peasy!"

Dominik paused. Even who knew what Sweet was capable of was amazed by her response. His teammates watched him intently, waiting for the end of the conversation.

"Really? Like that? Wow! How did you manage that?"

"Come to Atum's control room and I'll show you. It'll be easier. But you really should have figured it out by yourself."

"What should have I figured out by myself?"

But Sweet had hung up.

The supercomputer Atum that regulated Heliopolis was buried deep beneath the Palace. Osir and Sebek escorted Hexagon through the underground tunnels until they reached their destination, a vast natural cave that, like the rest of Heliopolis, blended Ancient Egyptian designs and futuristic technology.

Atum was the heart of Heliopolis and its home was not unlike a temple, except that there were holographic consoles instead of altars, giant magnetic screens instead of frescoes and busy technicians instead of priests. Atum drew its energy from geothermal wells and rejected its heat through channels leading to the surface.

Sweet was enthroned in the midst of this technological wonderland, sitting on a wide chair from which emerged luminous filaments connected directly to her body. Her eyes were white and her lips moved, as if she was dictating code. Dominik felt his heart clench at this spectacle. He had been so busy preparing for battle that he hadn't paid much attention to his girlfriend, and seeing her like this concerned him. Sweet had always preferred the company of machines to that of humans. Her obsession with artificial intelligence had sometimes been hampered by the limitations of their technology, but here, in the City of the Immortals, where science was so advanced that it appeared almost magical, those limitations no longer existed. Atum was like the Holy Grail the young woman had been searching for, and the Dark Flyer suddenly feared that she was lost to him forever.

Djehut, the scientist who had spent the day before with Sweet, ran towards Osir and the Hexagoneers as soon as he saw them.

"This is extraordinary!" he said. "The young mortal female communicates directly with Atum as none of us can, despite our psionic links! She saved hundreds of us during the attack just by repurposing our basic maintenance protocols..."

"Truly a day for wonders," said Osir.

Dominik was having his worst fears confirmed. Sweet had been utterly brilliant during the siege; he even owed her his life... But at what cost?

"Ah! There you are at last!"

Sweet's voice resounded throughout the room, coming from everywhere at once, even though her body hadn't moved.

"Sweet?" Cendrine wondered. "Is that you? Where are you?"

"Oh, I'm sitting comfy in that chair, fear not. But I'm also all around you and all over the city, too! I wish you could see what I see—the streams of data, the founts of knowledge, the..."

"Honey, can you please return to your body?" Dominik asked, a thin trickle of sweat running down his face. "It's really hard to speak to a disembodied voice."

"Oh, you spoilsport! But I guess it's okay... Fleshware has its uses too..."

There was a brief silence interspersed with some sputtering. Then Sweet's body shuddered, her eyes became clear again and she smiled at her friends.

The cables pulled away from her body; she shivered. Dominik wondered how long her consciousness had been merged with Atum... She stood up, at first a little wobbly on her legs, and approached the Hexagoneers. The Dark Flyer opened his arms and she welcomes his embrace with visible joy.

"So, you said you'd located Set?" Black Lys asked, eager to go on.

"Yeah... Well, no, not yet, but I know how to do it..."

Sweet went to a console and entered some instructions. A map of the world appeared on a large magnetic screen.

"We have to ways to find Set," she explained. "The first, as you pointed out, is to pinpoint the location of the equipment he stole from Melanos thanks to its characteristic Zhuvian characteristics. The other—which I prefer—relies on the fact that all Immortals have a unique psychic signature—some humans as well. Atum here has sensors that can detect any Immortal no matter where they are on Earth, even if they try to hide their presence..."

The young woman entered a line of code and a dot lit up on the map in Egypt.

"That's me," said Sweet. "Atum scanned me and can now find me wherever I am on Earth, and even though Heliopolis is in a Mirrorverse, strictly speaking, it is accurate enough to show my nearest location..."

"Wonderful, but what if Set isn't on Earth?" asked Blackie Sullivan.

"Then, we'll track him using the tech he stole from Melanos. But my gut instinct tells me he's still on our planet."

"Me, too," said the Archer. "But don't you need either Set's or Ra's psychic signatures first?"

"It would help, for sure, but it's not necessary," replied Sweet.

At that point, Djehut, who had been following the conversation, coughed with embarrassment. The Hexagoneers, who had almost forgotten his presence, turned to look at him.

"We do have the original Ra's psychic signature, but not that of Ben Leonard's—his current incarnation. As for Set and Athor, we had to purge theirs from Atum's mainframe in order to deny them access to it."

"However," said Osir, "the wise Tho had saved Ra's memories and genetic code in the Memory Vessel. When Ben Leonard first came to Heliopolis, it restored them into the young human."

Sweet's face lit up. She began to type in a frenzy.

"Thank you, Osir! That will make things so much simpler! Let's see. Everything in Heliopolis is connected to Atum, so I only need to locate that Memory Vessel... Ah, here it is! I'm downloading the information and sending it to my tracking program and *voilà*!"

Another bright spot had just lit up on the map— remarkably close to the first one... Sweet zoomed in on the location.

"The Valley of the Kings!" said the Black Lys.

"Next door, so to speak," said the Dark Flyer.

"Smart," said Rakar

"A classic move," concluded the Archer. "Hide as close as possible to your enemies."

Cendrine pulled herself together and began issuing orders.

"Fred, this time, we're going to try it your way. We're going to hit them *en masse* as hard as we can." Then she tuned to Osir and Sebek. "Regent, Captain, I know it's a lot to ask after what you've all been through, but can we still count on you?"

"Indeed! It will be an honor to fight with you again and go rescue my King—to honor or bury him!" Sebek replied. "I shall go with you, along with a few of my best men. The rest of our troops will keep watch over the city."

"We shall never abandon our rightful liege," added Osir. "In this war against Set, the Immortals of Heliopolis will fight alongside mighty Hexagon to the very end!"

CHAPTER XIII
The Book of the Dead

An almost unbearable stab of pain under his skull brought Ra out of his state of unconsciousness and back to a reality. He let out a groan before opening his eyes. He was still in the same small room, shackled to a metal seat. His blurred sight saw two silhouettes facing him: Amon, standing guard, and Set, his accursed brother, wearing an expression of joy and arrogance.

Ra recovered his lucidity and took a long breath. He raised his head with pride; it was out of the question for him to give Set the satisfaction of seeing him vanquished.

"I see that you're finally awake, dear brother," the evil Immortal observed. "You're just in time for your execution. It would have been a pity to miss that solemn event."

"Spare me your threats, you traitor!" Ben Leonard spat out. "If you're going to kill me, do it now, because you won't get another chance. Maybe this small victory will make up for the defeat you suffered at Heliopolis at the hands of Hexagon."

Set's features became distorted under the effect of anger. Ra was suddenly overwhelmed by another wave of pain while the psychic tentacles of his enemy struck at his mind.

"You naive fool! Do you really believe that I was defeated? On the contrary, I won! I took exactly what I wanted."

"Really? I thought you wanted to rule Heliopolis to avenge your exile. Don't try making your failure look like a victory!"

This time, Set let out a booming laugh. Ra hid his smile. As he planned, he was buying time by getting his brother to brag about his plans. He had never been able to resist it.

"I know what you're doing," replied the evil Immortal. "But I'm so convinced that there's nothing you can do anymore that I'll tell you my plan. And you will despair when you realize its grandeur and ineluctability."

Ra pretended to listen while sending discreet mental waves towards Amon.

"In order for you to fully grasp my genius," Set began, "I have to go back several millennia in the past, to the first time when I was looking for a way to kill you. You know that, in order to learn how to end your immortality, I traveled to the Realm of Shadows—Etarr's domain. At that time, my hatred for you was so great that even such a risky journey did not frighten me. It was that very hatred that enabled me to return alive from that Realm where the souls of the dead Immortals dwell. There, I questioned the Seven Ghosts and learned how to get rid of you.

"You know the rest. I killed our father to test the obsidian weapon capable of destroying an Immortal body and soul. Finally, I drove it into your heart and sent my men to storm the palace. I was the new King of Heliopolis! Alas, the scheming Tho saved your soul and found a way to preserve it through time. And the other Immortals overthrew me when Osir and Anhur started a rebellion. I was forced into exile with my faithful Athor...

"But my ambition was not sated, far from it! If Heliopolis did not want me, then I would conquer all the other divine kingdoms and the Earth, and would make this world the starting point for my conquest of the galaxy. But I was almost alone with few resources ... Then I hit upon an idea. In the Realm of Shadows, I had met the souls of many of our fellow Immortals, vaporous, drifting without purpose... But what if I could find a way to capture this dormant army and bend it to my will? What planet in the universe could stand up to thousands of mindless Immortals, immune to fear and pain, led by my unyielding will?

"My body was still imbued with the essence of the Realm of Shadows. I worked on it for centuries to discover the correct frequency that would enable me to bring the dead out of that dimension and back into ours—all under my control, of course. It was a long and difficult task, and I almost fell prey to discouragement more than once; but my hatred of Heliopolis always got me back to work. And at last I succeeded! I found a way to control the energies of the Realm of Shadows and locked it up in something I called the *Book of the Dead*. That shall ensure my dominance over this world, and all other worlds.

"But then an obstacle stood in my way: Moemi, a witch from the depths of Africa, whose command of the mystic arts was unparalleled. She introduced himself as the Protector of the Magic Sphere of the Earth and warned me about what I was trying to accomplish. According to her, breaking the barriers between this world and the Realm of Shadows and bringing dead Immortals back to life might plunge the entire cosmos into chaos. Of course, I turned a blind ear to her warnings! Instead, we fought: her spells and her magicks against my powers and my science. She was a worthy opponent, but I am Set! In the end, she was no match for me and I crushed her like an egg. However, she used her last ounce of strength to summon a mighty cosmic entity: the Guardian of the Threshold—a gargantuan figure with large wings, who seized my *Book of the Dead* and buried it inside a black hole at the other end of the universe, and there was nothing I could do to stop him! Then he went away, leaving me alone and defeated.

"I could not recreate the *Book* because I had infused it with all the residual Shadow Realm energies that I could extract from my body. And I couldn't return to Etarr's dimension because the risk of not being able to escape again was far too great. So I set out to find the black hole where the Guardian had locked up the *Book*. Athor and I traveled the cosmos and, after centuries of searching, I finally found it! But no one in this universe can venture into a black hole and return alive. It was the perfect trap! I spent centuries trying to solve it, gathering disciples around me. The barren worlds orbiting this black hole were soon filled by my followers.

"I knew there was only one object that could withstand the gravitational singularity: the Medallion of Ra. I returned to Earth determined to get my hands on it. But you know that part of the story: I discovered that my beloved brother, whom I had killed with my own hands, had returned to life into the body of a hapless mortal. I tried everything to destroy you and take the Medallion you wore. Alas, my plans all failed and you decided to return it to Heliopolis, where it was impossible for me to set foot.

"Once again, I wandered through time and space to find a solution and, in a parallel universe, I found Amon, whose power you beheld. Then, traveling to the negative

185

universe of Zhud, I secured the services of a colony of Xans. They're the ones who told me about Melanos and his advanced transdimensional technology. When I returned to Earth, the lovely Bastet joined me to spice up her long existence. She told me that the Gateway of the Gods had been scattered all over the world.

"Thanks to my allies, I was able to reassemble it and using Melanos' technology, launch an assault on Heliopolis where at last, I seized the Medallion of Ra. Now, I can retrieve the *Book of the Dead* and summon my army of ghostly Immortals!"

Ra regarded his brother with a mixture of horror and admiration. The depth of his hatred froze his blood, but he could not help admiring his exploits. To achieve his ambition, he had faced cosmic powers, subdues entire civilizations, traveled across the universe, ransacked Heliopolis, and even challenged an avatar of Death! How sad that such intelligence and courage wasn't employed in the service of nobler causes! If Set hadn't been insane, he would have certainly made an excellent king.

"This project of yours is pure folly," said Ra. "Blasphemy even! Why drag our fellow Immortals from their final resting place to quench your lust for power?"

"I won't let anything stand in my way!" replied Set. "You yourself will witness the return of our forefathers and feel utter despair before I finally terminate you!

The evil Immortal showed Ra the dagger with the obsidian blade that he immediately recognized for having felt it pierce his heart once in the past. Set slashed the skin of his neck with a cruel smile, drawing a trickle of blood, before taking a step back.

"There's one thing I still can't explain," Ra said. "Why attack New York? You didn't really need a diversion to steal the Eye of Udjat, and this reckless move put Hexagon on your tail."

"Ah, that... I've always kept an eye on you, brother. So when you joined this team, I knew you were looking for allies in anticipation of our next encounter. I attacked their city to assess their strength, nothing more. I recognized that they are indeed powerful, but still no threat to me."

All these deaths were just for a test... That was typical of Set, that's why he had to be stopped at all costs. Ra had gained some time, but if his brother reached his goal, even Hexagon would have no chance against an army of Immortals supported by Set's other forces.

"Come now, it's time for you to witness my triumph!" rejoiced the villain. "Enjoy the show, for it will be your last!"

Four faceless men entered the room and lifted the chair to which Ra was attached. Set led the way, Amon remaining behind them. The king of Heliopolis was transported through a series of corridors along which ran some electric cables before emerging into the open air.

They were on a vast plateau, which Ra recognized with a twinge of his heart. There, other faceless people were busy under Athor's watchful eye. The smooth-faced androids were assembling an imposing machine, a device within which the Gateway of the Gods, made up of the Eye of Udjat, the Ankh and the Scepter of Hekka, was powered by negative-fusion reactors. Advanced computers were connected to the machine and their screens displayed endless lines of calculations. Next to it, a massive cannon was pointed at the sky. Heavily armed Xans were patrolling the area as the sun was about to set. Bastet was walking around the site not bothering to hide her boredom.

Ra's seat was placed on the ground. Amon stood still at his side, ever the vigilant guardian. Set walked to the console and entered a set of coordinates.

"Is everything ready?" he asked.

"The universe awaits your will, master," nodded Athor.

The villain pressed a button and the transdimensional generator began to whirr, louder and louder. Sparks flew through the cables, and the Gateway of the Gods became surrounded with a blinding halo.

In the star-studded sky above, a hole opened with a tearing sound. It gradually widened until it almost blocked the entire horizon. Through it, Ra saw the black hole, attracting matter and particles to it. Orbiting around it was a barren planetoid on which a crowd had gathered. Many ships were cruising in its vicinity.

The mind—even that of an Immortal—could hardly grasp such a spectacle. Ra forced himself to watch. Set took the Medallion he had stolen from Heliopolis and placed it in the energy cell of a cannon, which was pointed at the black hole. The weapon was energized by this new source of power and the ground shook. A dense ray of pure white light burst out of the cannon and hit the black hole with a tremendous roar. The fury of a nova was meeting the abyss of a dead star and the cosmos itself seemed ablaze. An intense light filled the sky and everyone, even Set, had to lower their gaze.

When the spectators opened their eyes again, the black hole was gone. In its place floated countless debris, and among them a large cylinder covered with hieroglyphic circuit boards—the *Book of the Dead*.

On the planetoid, a blind priest raised his hands and summoned the artifact to him. The he vanished and reappeared at Set's side.

"Master, here is the instrument of your glory!" he said, kneeling respectfully.

The Immortal villain seized the *Book of the Dead* with unholy glee.

"At last! Look at me, brother!" he screamed at Ra. "Behold what I will now accomplish!"

Set brandished the cylinder like a scepter. The hieroglyphs lit up. The *Book of the Dead* opened and the energy of the Realm of Shadows gushed forth.

"Come to me, O Immortals who sleep in the arms of death!" invoked Set.

Shadows appeared on the ground, first crawling in clusters, then straightening up, taking human forms, translucent at the beginning, but becoming more and more refined. Ripped from their eternal sleep, the dead Immortals materialized in the world of the living! Ra felt his heart bleed as he recognized among them Kaor, the hero who had once died to save his soul...

"And now, for the final sacrifice!" Set screamed, turning toward his brother, a homicidal gleam in his eyes.

The villain approached Ra and raised his obsidian blade, ready to strike. But suddenly, an arrow snatched the weapon from his hands with extraordinary precision!

Set uttered a cry of surprise; the King of Heliopolis felt hope returning. He burst out laughing, as if to issue challenge to his accursed brother.

"Hexagon, forward!" shouted the voice of the Black Lys.

CHAPTER XIV
A Hero Found Again

The plan that the Black Lys had devised as the Hexajet covered the short distance between Mount Zefidu and Set's lair had unfolded perfectly and had allowed Hexagon to take their enemy by surprise and gain a crucial advantage in this new battle.

Blackie Sullivan's silhouette rose into the sky and positioned itself in front of the tear in the starry night sky. He stretched out his arms and summoned the dark energy that lurked beyond the portal, scattered remnants of the black hole that was there before the Medallion of Ra had destroyed it. The master of dark matter gorged himself with this energy until he himself became a singularity whose power was beyond comprehension. He uttered a long cry, whether of pain or drunkenness with power, he himself could not have said, and created a dark glowing sphere between his hands.

Then, Blackie directed his gaze towards a small valley, where the Xan ships that had survived the siege of Heliopolis, had landed, hidden from sight. He released the sphere, throwing it at the alien vessels without mercy.

The Xan were engulfed in an explosion of dark matter, a silent whirlwind that tore them apart. Trapped in this maelstrom, the alien ships disappeared without a trace. The valley turned into a perfect, smooth, round crater. In a single strike, Fred Sullivan had wiped out a war fleet.

He then turned towards the plateau and summoned all the power he had left, shaping it into a gravitational shock wave before releasing it towards Amon. The masked warrior was swept away and crashed into a cliff that collapsed, burying him under a shower of rocks.

Set moved away from Ra. The Xans and his faceless androids were joined by Athor, seeking to ensure his protection.

Suddenly, a series of arrows fell around Ra's chair. On each was a small cylinder from which an opaque vapor escaped. In a matter of seconds, the Hexagoneer was surrounded by a sense cloud of smoke.

Ben saw a figure appearing out of the smoke. It was Rakar, hidden under a cloaking spell. The Lakota shaman used his tomahawk to free his fellow Hexagoneer. Ra was finally able to stand up and massage his aching wrists. He felt his powers slowly returning to him, but his telepathy was still too weak to open a psychic channel between his teammates.

"Francis, you must bring me to Amon," he said eagerly. "I know who he really is; we mustn't fight him..."

The sound of an explosion interrupted them. Rising from under his pile of rocks, the masked warrior had taken off and hit Blackie Sullivan. Fred's aura of dark energy vanished upon contact and the two superhumans crashed to the ground. Without even getting up, Blackie Sullivan threw a violent punch at Amon, who responded with equal force. Once again, the two titans struggled with each other and the sounds of their blows shook the valley.

Rakar, still supporting Ra, moved with determination toward this apocalyptic battle.

Now the rest of the Heliopolis forces, which had silently encircled the plateau, appeared, shouting war cries. Sebek was leading the assault, directing a dozen veterans trained in combat whose psionic powers were as deadly as their determination.

Dominik Nero stood at their side, wearing a black Heliopolitan armor on which he had painted a red bird of prey. Though he had no superpowers, the Dark Flyer was an experienced fighter, and a potion the Immortals had given him temporarily increased his strength and endurance.

The soldiers massacred the disorganized ranks of the Xans. Sebek struck with the swiftness of a snake while his victims seemed to move in slow motion. Another Immortal wielding whips of psychic energy, as sharp as razors, cut off any opponent who dared to approach him. A third projected optical bursts of energy that swept the faceless androids away. Two more soldiers—twins—fought back to back: one burned the Xans in a deluge of flames, while the other turned them into ice statues.

A mighty shadow passed over the battlefield. It was the Hexajet, its machine guns mowing down the Xan reinforcements. Sweet was at the commands of the supersonic plane and tried to cover their advance as best as she could, worried that Dominik, who had insisted on going into battle without his hi-tech armor, might be injured. But he was the linchpin of Black Lys' plan. Sitting next to her was Isis the Healer, also anxious about her brother Sebek.

Step by step, the Immortals were making progress, driving the Xans and the androids away. Sebek had a precise target: Set! He intended to make the evil Immortal pay for all his crimes. His troops struck like a blade, taking no prisoners.

Black Lys and the Mysterious Archer were also trying to reach Set, but from behind. The Frenchwoman's energy blades struck relentlessly, destroying the strange, smooth-faced automatons, while the Archer's merciless arrows, fired at an almost unbelievable speed, mowed down the enemy reserves. There were only two of them, yet they they fought as if they were an entire army.

The Archer suddenly heard an evil cry, more like a hiss, and had just enough time to raise his bow to parry a merciless claw. Bastet had just pounced on him. Her usually beautiful face was distorted by a snarling, evil grimace. Jukka leaped back and fired five arrows, but the Immortal was too fast. She ran between them until she was close enough to engage in hand-to-hand combat. However, just as she prepared to strike again, Black Lys threw herself in front of her teammate, her blazing swords raised in defiance.

"You again!" spat the feline Immortal. "You have stood between me and my prey one too many time!"

Her claws ploughed through the air, but Black Lys only smiled and dodged the blow.

"Archer!" she shouted. "Deal with the Gateway! I'll take care of her. We have a score to settle."

The Finn hesitated only a second before obeying. He ran towards the Gateway of the Gods, firing his arrows to open himself a path. More androids surrounded Set's intricate machinery and reached out with their hands to blast him apart, but they were not as fast as Bastet. The Mysterious Archer never stopped running, avoided the blows, and mowed down the androids with his usual precision. However, he avoided firing arrows at the Immortals who'd been recalled from the Realm of Shadows.

When Jukka arrived at the cannon, he tore off Ra's Medallion and put it in his backpack. He did the same with the three artifacts powering the Gateway of the Gods. In their place, he dropped several explosive charges on a short timer. He then ran away as fast as he could and pressed a remote control. The targeted explosions destroyed the controls, the computers, and the generators. Set's mighty engines of death were now only a smoking heap of rubble.

The consequences were immediate: the tear in the sky that connected Earth to a distant section of the universe closed up. The ships on the other side—Set's galactic army of conquest—failed to cross the rift before it closed and remained trapped thousands of light years away.

Suddenly, an unexpected blow sent the Mysterious Archer rolling to the ground. He straightened up and spotted his attacker: an alien priest with dead eyes. Jukka pulled out his tonfas and prepared for another fight.

"No one opposes the will of the master!" spat the blind man.

Without answering, the Archer launched himself into an attack mode. He struck left and right, but the priest blocked him easily without even looking at him. Jukka deduced that, if truly blind, he relied on his other overdeveloped senses. Also, this strange being used a type of martial art that the Archer had never seen before, and was therefore unpredictable. He knew that he couldn't let that fight go on forever. After a few minutes, he was able to direct their battle closer to the fire that was now ravaging Set's machinery. The roar of the flames, their heat, and the smell of burned components filled the air and distorted the blind priest's attacks. His moves were now more hesitant and flawed.

The Archer took advantage of this to strike. He waited patiently for a metal plate to twist under the effect of heat and crash with a tremendous noise to deliver his fatal blows. The tonfas whirled and hit the priest's grey flesh hard. The alien fell to his knees, out of breath. A harder blow on the back of his neck caused him to fall to the ground, unconscious.

Meanwhile, the Black Lys' mind was like her swords—sharp, full of energy, and with an unparalleled cutting edge. She emptied her mind to let her body use the full extent of her art, learned through years of training. Her brain was merely a relay between her senses and her limbs. Her blades danced in the air with fierce joy.

Facing her, Bastet was foaming with rage. Swift and agile beyond human norms, the Immortal was quick to strike with her sharp claws—and strike to kill. But all her assaults were met y the blazing blades of the Hexagoneer. Yes, Cendrine's body was now covered with cuts and scrapes, but no mortal blow ever reached her. The swordswoman chose to remain on the defensive, knowing that each of her feints, each of her evasions, only increased the Immortal's anger. And the more angry she became, the more confused and clumsy her attacks were.

"How can you, a mere mortal, stand up to me?" Bastet raved. "I've lived centuries, I'm more experienced than you!"

"More experienced?" Cendrine replied without losing her focus. "Your technique is poor; you rely only on your physical abilities. You're little more than a dilettante who thinks that her long life makes her superior! I've been training since I was a baby to perfect my art. I am the best fencer on Earth!"

Now, the Black Lys decided she could launch a counterattack. No more parries and dodges: she slipped under Bastet's guard and set about showing her the full extent of her skills. And, despite her speed, despite her skill, despite her strength, the Immortal was overwhelmed. The bio-electric blades cruelly bit into her flesh and repeatedly spilled her blood. For the first time in her very long life life, Bastet knew fear...

"Let me show you what the skills and will of a mere mortal can do," said the silver-haired Frenchwoman.

The Black Lys adopted her favorite stance, blades crossed in front of her, then attacked. Her swords sliced through the air, drawing intricate curves with incomparable speed. Cendrine de Mérignan's most secret trick was known as the *Botte d'Altotas*, a complex blow the secret of which had been taught to her ancestor, Lucas de Mérignan, by his Master in the 18th century. It was a devastating blow of formidable power that could not be countered. Bastet was unable to protect herself and ended up stabbed in the chest. Had she been human, she would have dropped dead at once. Instead, humiliated, she curled up and tried to protect herself by raising her arms in front of her face.

The Black Lys decided o have mercy and, instead of decapitating her foe, crossed her energy blades again and delivered a final blow meant only to stun that sent the Immortal crashing to the ground, utterly defeated.

Cendrine caught her breath. Around her, the strange opalescent mist that Set had invoked was producing ever more new silhouettes. There were now more than a hundred of them, and some had acquired a disturbing density.

The Black Lys wandered between the materializing Immortals and headed towards Set.

Ra and Rakar could barely approach Blackie Sullivan and Amon. The two fighters struck each other with blows of incredible power. Their impacts sent shock waves all around them. Ra groaned. He knew that Amon had to be freed from Set's control in order to return Jeff Sullivan to the team. But the struggle between the two brothers was too violent to attempt anything.

Blackie Sullivan had to admit that he had never been tested so hard by any of his past opponents. It wasn't so much Amon's strength that made the difference—they were about equal—as his robotic way of fighting. The masked warrior acted like a machine, striking without any consideration for his own health. His fists bled, his bones, but he didn't stop. It was as if he felt no pain, knew no doubt. The master of dark matter, deprived of the Soul of Levan, could not fight like this; he held back his punches in order to not to hurt himself, but that was enough to widen the gap between them...

Above all, Fred Sullivan felt an intense sense of familiarity with Amon. He knew him: of that, he was certain. But his foe's expressionless mask prevented him from seeing his true face. Several times Blackie struck it with his fist, but it didn't break. Finally, he grabbed his opponent from behind, pressing on his neck with his arm in a relentless grip. With his other hand, he grabbed the mask and tried to tear it off, but Amon held his wrists and stopped him. Blackie's muscles tensed, ready to burst, his face twisting under the stress...

Suddenly, Amon took off and flew backwards, his opponent still clinging to his back. He hit the cliff just behind them. Blackie had to let go and fell to the ground as the mute warrior landed at a safe distance.

Ra realized that this was the opportunity he had been waiting for.

"Rakar, listen to me," he said. "I don't have time to explain, but I need you to create a diversion. Use one of your spells to damage Amon's mask. That's his weak spot. Strike as hard as you can and I'll take care of the rest."

The Lakota shaman wasted no time. He trusted his teammate and rushed towards Amon. The masked warrior struck at him, but his fists encountered only emptiness. Rakar had thrown himself to the ground in and struck his opponent in the thigh with the blade of his cutlass.

Ra ran towards Blackie Sullivan who was just recovering from his shock. He supported him as best he could and discovered with some dread that the master of dark matter had been injured: his face was blue, one of his eyes was so swollen that it was almost completely closed, his lips were red with blood... Yet, he was ready to continue the fight.

"Fred," Ra explained, "Rakar is buying us time, but he won't last long. He should be able to damage the mask, but then, it's up to you. I'll throw you back at Amon with whatever telekinetic power I have left so you can finish breaking it off. But you'll only get one shot. Do you understand me?"

Blackie wiped his mouth and nodded. Drawing on his last resources, he straightened up and waited for the right moment.

Rakar was in constant motion. He knew that a single blow from Amon could kill him, so he had to dodge his opponent and watch for an opening. Finally, he found it. Amon seemed invulnerable, but in reality, he wasn't. He, too, had been injured in the fight against Blackie Sullivan. Suddenly, the Lakota warrior jumped up and raised his tomahawk. The weapon came down in a flash and hit the golden mask, which cracked sharply. Amon put one hand to his wounded face and swept Rakar off his feet.

Ra exploded with psychic energy. Blackie Sullivan, bathed in an aura as bright as the sun, took off like a rocket. He hit Amon at a speed close to that of sound and put all his strength and determination into a single blow. His fist struck and the golden mask which shattered into a thousand pieces, sending Amon crashing fifteen yards away. Blackie then hit the ground, almost unconscious.

The now maskless Amon rose up with hesitant gestures. His face was turned towards the Hexagoneers and, as they beheld it, they all felt their hearts skipping a beat.

"Impossible!" Rakar whispered.

"Now, I understand," said Blackie Sullivan, still on the ground, leaning on his elbow.

In front of them stood Jeff Sullivan, the Man of Brass—he who had given his life on the Moon to save mankind from the folly of the Necromancer—one of the founding members of Hexagon—Fred's own brother!

Jeff took three steps forward, still staring blankly. Then, he grabbed his head in his hands, as if his mind was twisted by intense pain. Ra played his last card: using his telepathy, he widened the breach he had felt in the soul of Amon in order to allow Jeff's own soul to reemerge. He bombarded him with memories, every-thing he knew about the Man of Brass.

Then he senses a great golden light bursting out of the darkness and driving him away.

Jeff Sullivan was back!

The Xans and the faceless androids were lying all over the battlefield. Set's army, already diminished after the siege of Heliopolis, was now reduced to a handful of soldiers huddling around their master. The alien forces that had been massed on the other side of the Gateway of the Gods could no longer come as reinforcements.

Sebek and his men surrounded the evil Immortal. The Black Lys, the Mysterious Archer and the Dark Fly-er stood at their side. The Hexajet had landed on a near-by plateau so that Isis could come and heal the wounded. Victory had been won.

Set had his head down, as if he was ready to surren-der. Sebek stepped forward and the Xans pulled away in front of him.

"It's over, traitor!" aid the brave captain. "You un-derestimated the combined forces of Heliopolis and Hexagon. Now, end to your accursed plan and send our brothers back to their eternal sleep."

Set remained perfectly silent. Then his shoulders shook and he let out a loud, uncontrollable laugh. His eyes rolled wildly. Everyone stepped back, as if fright-ened by this sudden explosion of madness.

"Over?" shouted Set. "Oh, no, Sebek, it's not over, In fact, it's just beginning. Your pitiful attack will allow me to test my new army against you—and destroy all my fiercest enemies in one fell swoop!"

Set raised his arms and his body let out a greenish mist, which spread over the entire plateau and mingled with the dead Immortals. For the first time, they stepped forth, moving towards the Hexagoneers and the soldiers of Heliopolis, their empty gaze now filled with an emerald spark.

The proud Immortals of yesteryear were now the thralls of Set!

Jeff Sullivan stood there in a daze. He looked around him and didn't understand what was going on. Blackie ignored the pain and went to meet him as a flood of emotion rippled through him.

"Fred?" asked Jeff in a surprised voice.

"Yes, it's me," confirmed the master of dark matter. "Look, Jeff, it's complicated, so I'll give you the short version. I'm on your side, I'm with Hexagon now. As for you, you've been min-controlled by a madman who turned you into a living weapon..."

"I don't understand... I was... somewhere else, then suddenly..."

Ra approached with Rakar.

"If I may, I will meld our minds," he suggested, "so that explanations can be given without wasting time."

The Immortal opened a psychic channel between the four of them and immediately the memories of each man flowed in and were shared. Rakar and Blackie Sullivan witnessed the long struggle of the Man of Brass on the world of the Flyers, until he met Set. Jeff got a glimpse of Hexagon's adventures since his death on the Moon. The memories remained a little confused at first because there was so much to assimilate.

"So you now carry the Soul of Levan?" Jeff asked Fred.

"It was logical after what happened to you. But when we are close, it sort of fades away, as if it's confused by the simultaneous presence of two heirs..."

Jeff Sullivan raised his hands and made fists.

"I don't feel the Soul in me anymore, but I am still the Man of Brass."

Rakar stepped forward and warmly shook Jeff's hand.

"It is such a joy to see you alive again!" he said. "I can't wait to tell Mary and Kathryn."

"Are they all right?" Jeff eagerly interrupted him.

"They're perfectly safe, at home, together."

"We shall soon join them," said Fred. "It feels as if we won this battle."

"I wouldn't be so sure," said Ra, sounding unsure.

Around them, the dead Immortals, bathed in the green energy emitted by Set, stared at the Hexagoneers. Some were glowing, already tapping into their own psionic powers, ready to attack.

The battle wasn't over yet!

CHAPTER XV
The Realm of Shadows

Instinct took over. Jeff and Fred Sullivan took up fighting positions against the dead Immortals. Although they were both wounded, they were ready to fight another fight.

Jeff grabbed one of the Immortals and threw him at another. Then, he took off and, flying low, sent many of them crashing to the ground. Despite the fatigue and the pain, he used all his strength to put as many their opponents out of action as possible...

Blackie rushed in after his brother. He threw punches and knocked down anyone who tried to attack them. Stamping his foot on the ground, he caused a small earthquake causing the Immortals who were pressing him too close to stumble and fall.

Nevertheless, the fight remained unequal. The newly-resurrected Immortals were too many and felt no pain, no fatigue, no doubt. They used their powers and struck the two Sullivans with all their powers. At this rate, they would not last very long.

Despite his exhaustion, Ra decided to help his allies, but, as he prepared to jump into the fray, Rakar held him back.

"Wait, Ben. It won't do any good for you to collapse," said the shaman.

"But we can't let them get slaughtered!" cried the Immortal.

"Of course not! But I have a plan, and I need you to implement it."

Ra listened to Rakar.

"You told us about the Realm of Shadows and its ruler—Etarr the Inevitable," continued the Lakota. "Do you think this entity knows about Set's plans and actions?"

The Immortal thought for a moment.

"No, probably not," he answered. "Etarr is an avatar of Death, a powerful but not omniscient entity. He is jealous of his prerogatives and would not let his subjects escape him that. But he sometimes falls asleep and he likely doesn't know what Set has done..."

" Good. What if I went into the Realm of Shadows and told him? I imagine he still has some kind of hold over these dead Immortals?"

"Yes... I suppose he does… It's possible..." Ra hesitated. "But I could barely escape from his dimension when Set sent me there once. You could become trapped in it forever!"

Rakar had a determined smile.

"Don't underestimate me. The magic of my people runs in my veins. Besides, I'm counting on you to open a psychic link between us—like a lifeline."

Ra thought that Rakar's idea was risky, but feasible. Besides, they were running out of options.

"Still," the Immortal remarked, "how are you going to get to the Realm of Shadows?"

"You've been there yourself, as you just said," replied the shaman. "The energies of that dimension still permeate you. I will use them as a guide."

"Very well," said Ra. "But let me warn the others first."

The King of Heliopolis used his powers to linked all the Hexagoneers together.

"*Ben, are you all right?*" asked the Black Lys. "*Set has thrown all these dead Immortals at us and we may not last long.*"

"*Same here, but Rakar has a plan. You all need to hold on for a few minutes longer.*"

"*Try to hurry,*" interjected the Dark Flyer. "*We're at the end of our rope.*"

"*We will stand,*" said the Mysterious Archer, "*but we're counting on you.*"

Ra turned towards Rakar.

"I'm ready," said the shaman.

The two men sat face to face. The Immortal created a strong mental bond between him and Rakar, while the Lakota chanted softly—an incantation designed to strengthen his mind for the astral journey he was about to undertake.

A grey swirl of vapors rose from the body of the King of Heliopolis and Rakar breathed them in. His eyes turned white as his body stiffened. Ra felt their bond being stretched to the extreme. Then Rakar's soul plunged into the abyss...

A feeling of infinite fall.

A shrill scream.

Lights flashing.

A strong smell of putrefaction.

A taste of ashes.

Rakar suddenly woke up. He leapt to his feet, weapons in hand, ready to defend himself.

But there was no one there.

He was in a putrid swamp: ponds of mud stirring with strange eddies; twisted, bent trees rustling despite the absence of wind; a spongy ground disgorging brack-ish water...

Everything was dead or dying. Yet a few signs of life remained: strange insects buzzing; a lizard drinking from a foul puddle...

Rakar's senses were dulled by the Realm of Shadows. He sensed that a new torpor trying to creep into his mind, the irrepressible desire to let go, to stop struggling, to fall into a death-like sleep... He shook his head to chase away these feelings and drew on his mental link with Ra—and the world of the living.

The Immortal stood firm; Rakar knew he could count on him. Yet, even this was not enough to dispel the deathly call that emanated from the Realm of Shadows. He had to keep struggling, drawing images of life, such as his companion Kathryn, so beautiful and flamboyant; his unborn children, beautiful twins; Jeff Sullivan, finally back among them; his teammates who had full confidence in him... Eventually, the torpor passed and his will was strengthened.

Rakar tried to orient himself, but found no landmarks. The sky was uniformly grey and no sun was shining. The atmosphere was neither hot, nor cold. The shaman set out to find Etarr. He walked through the swamp for what seemed like hours, but he knew that his perception of time was likely twisted. His mental link with Ra ensured that he did not become disoriented. He knew that only a few minutes had passed since he had arrived there.

Along the way, Rakar encountered other Immortals. All were motionless, expressionless, yet a feeling of deep sadness emanated from them. There was a melancholy that tried to capture his spirit and he had to fight to cancel its power; yet, he could not help but feel compassion for these beings endowed with eternal existence, but condemned to a living death. Rakar knew that the souls of mortals did not perish when they died but followed a cycle of incarnations, very different from what the Immortals' fate. No doubt it was the price they paid for the considerable gifts they had during their lifetime.

He saw the bodies of some Immortals blur, become evanescent and then rise up into the sky like smoke. It was the spell used by Set to call them back into the world of the living. But there were still hundreds of them left in the Realm of Shadows. The army that Set was assembling would make him invincible!

The shaman felt anger grow within him: the final rest of the soul was a sacred notion, and what Set was doing an unspeakable blasphemy. His determination to stop the evil Immortal became all the greater for it. Addressing a mute greeting to the remaining Immortals, he resumed his search for of Etarr.

Eventually, he came out of the swamps and crossed a forest, then a desert, and finally arrived at a city in ruins. None of this followed any logic, but there he was, standing in front of a massive temple, covered with vines embedded between its stones. An imposing colonnade framed a doorway beyond which reigned a cold and silent darkness.

The shaman knew at once that he had reached the end of his quest, but the trickiest part was still to come. He entered the temple and found himself in the center of a vast circular room with a floor paved with a half-erased mosaic. Along the walls, countless candleholders stood vigil. The flames of their candles gradually became brighter, casting a diffuse glow throughout the room.

Unlike Ozark, his fellow Lakota and Earth's current supreme sorcerer, Rakar was not accustomed to dealing with cosmic entities. Yet, he had to negotiate with Etarr to save his friends—and Earth.

"O mighty Etarr!" he called out.

Nothing happened. Rakar stood still, opened his mind and expanded his perceptions.

"O mighty Etarr, I implore you!" he repeated. "Hear my prayer here and now—for soon, it will be too late!"

Suddenly, the candles started burning with increased intensity. The ground shook. The air became murkier...

Rakar felt it before he saw it: a colossal force, a being of celestial proportions, an inflexible will, a malignant intelligence... Etarr was suddenly there, and his essence filled the whole room.

The shaman stilled his heart. This entity personified death; it exuded putrefaction and despair and inevitability.

An immense face with inhuman features, a cold and inquisitive look, materialized in front of him—Etarr! He was the embodiment of the Realm of Shadows, the wrathful jailer of the dead Immortals.

"Who dares disturb my rest?" Etarr asked and his voice echoed all around.

The shaman knelt down, adopting the most humble posture possible. A cold sweat froze his skin. There was no room for error.

"I am Rakar of the Lakota, O mighty Etarr," he replied. "I am the bearer of ill tidings."

The floating face lit up with a pale glow of curiosity.

"Strange. My subjects have no free will, and yet here you are, speaking to me..."

"I am not one of your subjects," replied Rakar. "Indeed, I do not belong in your domain. I am but a mortal from the world of the living."

The face showed what might have been surprise.

"I see. Speak then! Explain what brought you here."

Rakar moistened his lips. This was it.

"Ill tidings, as I said, Dreaded One," he said. "Do you not feel the disturbance in your kingdom? What is being stolen from you as I speak?"

The face of Etarr seemed for a moment to be plunged into a deep introspection. Then, it spoke again:

"Yes... I feel it now... My subjects are being taken away... one by one! Who dares desecrate my Realm? Challenge my will?"

"A brazen Immortal called Set," replied Rakar, "who already ventured once into your domain to steal your secrets. Now he claims to rule over the dead Immortals and recalls them to stand among the living to enforce his will."

"It must not be!"

Etarr's face became twisted with anger.

The shaman sensed the awakening of a cosmic power so vast that even he could not imagine its magnitude.

That power split into innumerable threads that bonded with the soul of each of the dead Immortals who inhabited the Realm of Shadows. Then, it traveled further, breaking down the barriers between dimensions, and touched all those whom Set had gathered.

Then Etarr mobilized his will, and Rakar felt more than he heard numerous spectral howls—the cries of pain of those Immortals caught between two worlds, pulled between the call of their sovereign and Set's unholy control.

Rakar sought to cover his ears, but these laments reached his soul directly. He cried out in turn as he felt with every fiber of his body the pain of the lost Immortals, who had become the stake in this abominable struggle.

Then, it all stopped. The shaman got up with difficulty, almost losing his balance. Everything was silent. Etarr's energy had dissipated. But his face still floated above.

"My rule has been restored," said the entity. "Now I will send you back to the Living. Your presence here is not... desirable."

The eyes of Etarr the Inevitable emitted a white radiance that enveloped Rakar. He was lifted from the ground and rose until he was thrown through the veil of dimensions. He clung with all his strength to the psychic link that Ra maintained between them in order not to get lost between realities.

The feeling of crashing to the ground.

Exclamations of joy.

The soft darkness of the night sky.

The crisp air of an Egyptian night.

The flavor of life.

Rakar awoke, supported by Ra.

"You did it, my friend!" the Immortal enthused.

All around them, the world was bathed in a mist that was gradually sinking into the ground.

CHAPTER XVI
Set Defeated

A little while ago, Jeff and Fred Sullivan stood back to back, surrounded by a swarm of dead Immortals. The two brothers were fighting side by side for the first time in their lives. It was a small consolation as death was near. Their opponents concentrated their psychic powers to crush them both with one last blow.

"If only I had access to dark matter," Blackie regretted bitterly.

"The Soul of Levan has abandoned us at the worst possible moment," added the Man of Brass. "Still, no matter what happens now, I'm glad I could count you among my friends at last!"

Fred grunted an assent, but his fierce smile said it all. If the Sullivans were to disappear today, it would not be without a last moment of glory!

As the Immortals rushed around to finish them off, the two heroes gathered their last ounces of strength for one final showdown.

But suddenly, Set's puppets stopped their movements. An expression of intense suffering appeared on their faces and a collective scream escaped from their throats.

They fell to their knees and began writhing in pain on the ground as their bodies lost substance. The vaporous energy that had taken them into our world was now summoning them back and they were literally dissolving.

Driven by his usual compassion, Jeff knelt beside an Immortal and took her hand. She seemed lost, didn't understand what was happening to her. The green spark had vanished from her eyes, to be replaced by a glimmer of despair.

The Man of Brass held her until she had completely disintegrated, replaced by an unhealthy mist that covered the ground before sinking deep into it.

Blackie put a hand on his shoulder as Ra arrived, supporting a weakened Rakar.

"There was nothing we could do," said the master of dark matter. "They were already dead. They just went back to where they belonged."

"Fred is right," Ra confirmed. "Set disturbed their sterna rest to turn them into his puppets. He's the only one to blame."

"That was... a horrible place," Rakar whispered. "I don't know how you people can live with the expectation of such a fate."

The Immortal smiled sadly.

"The Realm of Shadows is an unattractive place, but some of us think that it is only a intermediate place, a kind of purgatory if you will, before a new existence. I confess I'm in no hurry to test that theory."

"Let's rejoin the others," Jeff suggested. "And deliver this Set to the justice of Heliopolis!"

Ra nodded. He had had to use all of his powers to maintain a connection with Rakar, and had had therefore to cut his psychic channel with the other Hexagoneers. He hoped that they were all safe.

When Set's dead Immortals had first come to life, confusion had reigned among the soldiers of Heliopolis. It was traumatic for them to see former members of their people turn against them, and an abominable blasphemy to be forced to fight them.

As always, Sebek set an example and came out of his stupor with a war cry filled with rage. He leapt upon the ghosts and struck many with his sword. His soldiers followed him with tears in their eyes.

Dominik Nero was among them, also armed with a sword. He threw himself into the fray with fervor, the anger of his comrades-in-arms having won him over. The Black Lys and the Mysterious Archer exchanged a quick glance and set out to carve a path towards Set.

The villain was taking advantage of the chaos to retreat towards his base. Jukka and Cendrine struck mercilessly, and many Immortals fell before them, but being dead already, they rose again! They had been taken away from the Realm of Shadows and Set's *Book of the Dead* forced them to stay on Earth and fight for its master.

Athor faced the two Hexagoneers to protect his master's escape. He spread his arms and his gaze turned dark. At once, the Black Lys and the Archer found themselves on a vast icy plain beaten by polar winds. The illusion was perfect: they could feel the cruel bite of the cold, hear the roar of the storm, watch the endless icy expanse that lay ahead of them. Cendrine was disoriented for a moment, but the Archer had already fought Athor's powers before. He had memorized every detail of the plateau to perfection before the attack had begun, and calmly and confidently shot an arrow.

"Your tricks don't work on me," he said.

The veil of illusion tore as the arrow hit Athor in the shoulder. The Immortal whirled on himself under the force of the impact and collapsed, groaning in pain. The Black Lys breathed a sigh of relief.

"That leaves only Set," she said.

"Let me give you a hand," Dominik intervened.

The Dark Flyer, attired in an Heliopolitan armor, had broken away from Sebek's troops and rejoined them. Cendrine looked at him concerned.

"Are you sure you're up to it?" she asked.

"Sweet seems to think so," he said to reassure her.

She nodded and stepped aside to let him pass. The Mysterious Archer gave her a discreet sign to wish her good luck. The two Hexagoneers positioned themselves to protect their comrade, blocking the Immortals who were already advancing towards them.

Dominik Nero carried a heavy legacy. His father had not only bequeathed him his company—the powerful multinational NeroTek—but also the title of Dark Flyer. The young man had often felt overwhelmed by these responsibilities. He couldn't help wonder if he was up to the task. He had proven his abilities fighting alongside Hexagon for quite a few years now, but he had lost against Starlock and the Salamandrite known as "Glory" in Haiti,[12]

Still, Dominik was a genius who had more than perfected the arsenal bequeathed by Cletus Nero to the team. He had created the Dark Flyer's armored suit and unlocked the secret of hexagonium. He had never fled or abandoned his companions. Even without his armor and gadgets, he was an accomplished athlete and talented fighter.

His relationship with Sweet had sublimated his qualities. She complemented him wonderfully and made him want to surpass himself. She always found the solution to every problem. To neutralize Set, she had come up with a plan. And Dominik had insisted on being her instrument.

---

[12] See *Strangers* #2.

Set was running ahead of him, but Dominik was stronger and faster. He caught up with the evil Immortal in a few strides, jumped on top of him and tackle him to the ground. The two men rolled around in the dust. Set was trying to push off the attacker and Dominik to immobilize his foe. After a brief struggle, the Dark Flyer straddled the deceitful Immortal and held his wrists to the ground.

"It's over!" he said. "Send your ghosts back where they came from or I swear I'll slit your throat."

"You're mad!" spat Set. "You're a mere mortal; you can't handle me..."

Dominik then felt the Immortal's mind creep into his. Suddenly, the pain came, searing and deep. He became nauseous and rolled to the ground, holding his head in his hands. His face was distorted by pain.

"You're helpless without your armor, Dark Flyer," Set boasted. "Yes, I can see right through you! You still live in your father's shadow..."

"Get... out... of... my... head!" moaned Dominik.

"Not until I've destroyed you! You will pay for daring to raise your hand against me! Ah! I see here a spark of joy, one that allows you to combat all your doubts—a woman... What if I destroyed every last memory of her? It would be as if she had never existed for you. Your psyche will collapse without her to sustain it..."

Set concentrated and found the area in Dominik's mind where the Dark Flyer stored all his memories related to Sweet. He cast his psychic tentacles, aiming to destroy everything... before he realized he was trapped!

Tiny mental waves surrounded this part of Dominik's mind and clung to the projection of Set's. They multiplied and invaded the soul of the evil Immortal. It was now Set's turn to scream as his head was filled with an infernal tumult.

The Dark Flyer raised his head with a triumphant smile. He stood up and dusted off his armor.

"You didn't expect that, did you?" he said, his voice dripping with irony. "Let me tell you how we got you. I hear you like to tell your plans before your intended victims, so allow me to do the same. The beautiful young woman you saw in my mind is called Sweet, and she's a lot smarter than you. Using the supercomputer of Heliopolis, she developed psychospores—like computer viruses for the mind..."

Set was now on his knees. His nose and ears were bleeding; a continuous moaning was coming out of his mouth, from which a steady trickle of saliva dripped. He stared at the Dark Flyer with a look full of hatred.

"I'm not as good at science as she is, but I do have a few skills myself," Dominik continued. "So I volunteered for her to implant in my mind these psychospores she had designed specifically to neutralize you. Of all the Hexagoneers, I was the ideal prey for you. As you said, without my armor, I don't count for much. But you forgot that my real power is my mastery of science and technology. So you got inside my head and got infected!"

Still cowering on the ground, Set could no longer hear the Dark Flyer's words. He was plunged into a deep, painful trance in which his mind was saturated. The psychospores would eventually dissipate in a couple of hours, but until then, the Immortal was helpless.

"Remember this, Set: you were defeated by two mere mortals," Dominik concluded.

Then he lifted Set's body and threw him across his shoulder.

He heard cries of victory and deduced that the ghosts from the Realm of Shadows were no longer a threat. He didn't know if his defeat of the evil Immortal was the cause of it, but rejoiced nevertheless and set out to join his comrades.

Victory had come as suddenly as it did unexpectedly. The Black Lys, the Mysterious Archer, Sebek and his men had been fighting foot to foot with little hope of success when suddenly, the dead Immortals had stood still and, all together, uttered an unbearable scream.

Collapsing on the ground, one after the other, they had disintegrated quickly, their bodies unraveling into misty filaments, who had quickly sunk into the ground.

In less than a minute, there was nothing left of them on the plateau, except a fine mist stagnating at ground level.

The Black Lys smiled at the Mysterious Archer.

"It looks as if Ben and Francis succeeded," she said.

"I never doubted it," replied the Finn. "I was only hoping that they would do so before we all perished."

Sweet and Isis arrived and the Immortal Healer went to attend to her brother and the wounded soldiers. Sweet scanned the plateau with a worried look in her eyes.

"Where's Dominik?" she asked. "I hope he didn't decide to play hero without thinking..."

"As if it were in my habit not to think!" said a voice behind her.

The Dark Flyer stepped out from behind a rock and laid his burden—Set—on the ground, where the evil Immortal joined his cohort, Athor.

He breathed a long sigh of relief. Sweet threw herself into his arms and embraced him tenderly.

"You idiot!" she said. "It was a risky plan..."

"I never doubted you and I was sure it would work."

Coming from the other side of the plateau, the last Hexagoneers joined their teammates. Night had fallen and only their silhouettes could be seen. The Black Lys waved at them.

Ra was supporting Rakar, while a battered Blackie Sullivan walked next to...

Cendrine's heart suddenly stopped. No, it wasn't possible! Could it be...?

"You're not dreaming, Cendrine, it's I!" said Jeff Sullivan.

"Welcome back, brother!" said the Mysterious Archer who had perceived the truth.

"But... how...?" said Dominik, flabbergasted.

Jeff hugged Cendrine who hugged him back as if to prevent him from disappearing again. Her tears flowed uncontrollably. The Man of Brass held her close to him while Dominik and Jukka surrounded him and nagged him with questions.

"I'm sorry I caused you so much pain," said Jeff. "But I'm back now."

"When we are rested, I will share all our memories," Ra said, "so that all the questions you have will be answered. But for now, I think it s enough to rejoice in our victory."

Sebek looked at Jeff Sullivan with suspicion. For him, he was still Amon, who had killed the general. But he decided to trust the Hexagoneers for the time being. However, he was determined to hold this mysterious individual accountable.

"We have captured Set, Athor and Bastet," said the captain to Ra. "I propose to take them back to Heliopolis so that they may be judged there."

Ra agreed.

Supporting each other, the Hexagoneers headed for the Hexajet while the Immortals prepared to return to Heliopolis. Exhausted, they all were nevertheless happy to have triumphed, especially since there was so much at stake. And all were eager to enjoy a well-deserved rest in the City of the Gods.

None of them noticed that the fine mist that curled at their feet, far from disappearing into the Earth, was now drawing strange arabesques on the ground...

CHAPTER XVII
The Wrath of Etarr

Rakar felt his hair stand up as an icy shiver ran down his spine. His mystical sixth sense caused him to make a muffled groan.

"Are you all right?" asked Ra who was still supporting him on their way to the Hexajet.

"No," whispered the shaman. "I sense a threat nearby..."

The Immortal took a quick glance at their prisoners—Set, Athor and Baste—still guarded by the soldiers of Heliopolis, their wrists tightly bound.

"One last gift from my brother?" he worried.

"No. Worse than that," Rakar replied.

The whole group stopped. Now everyone could feel the disturbance. It was as if the air itself was charged with electricity.

"What's going on?" asked the Black Lys.

"Damn it! It's never over, is it!" Dominik complained.

They formed a circle to optimize their defense, keeping their prisoners in the center. On the plateau, now lit by a pale moon, they saw nothing but the wrecks of their battle, the transdimensional generator reduced to rubble and the dislocated bodies of the faceless androids. Yet, their sense of unease was growing; a primal fear and insidious despair crept into the minds.

"It's the mist," suddenly remarked the Archer.

At their feet, the vaporous filaments appeared as if they were driven by a strange will. This mist had come with the Immortals summoned by the *Book of the Dead*, and should have gone when they returned to the Realm of Shadows. Yet, it was still there and its density was increasing. The opalescence rose in thick volutes and soon bathed the entire plateau in its opaque whiteness.

A smell of putrefaction assailed their nostrils—it was the scent of death itself. Through the mist, they started seeing a changing, distant, half-transparent landscape, a dark forest, a putrid swamp, a rocky desert, a long plain with yellowed grass...

"It's the Realm of the Shadows," said Rakar, recognizing the scenery from his astral journey.

No sooner had he uttered these words than some of the mist rose up and formed the inhuman face of Etarr the Inevitable!

At this vision, the Immortals froze; even Ra felt a bead of icy sweat run down his back.

"Impossible," muttered the King of Heliopolis.

The floating figure came to life as its eyes sparkled.

"I am Etarr the Inevitable! I hereby claim this world and its inhabitants as mine. The Realm of Shadows will merge with it so that my essence can take full possession of it."

The ground began to shake, at first lightly, then harder. A stridence echoed over the whole plateau. The mist rose again and merged with the clouds, before gradually spreading in all directions. The reflections of the Realm of Shadows became more tangible as Etarr's power started spreading.

Ra advanced, his arms spread out as a sign of humility.

"O mighty Etarr, I beseech thee to renounce thy purpose," he pleaded. "The clash between our worlds could destroy both, and threaten the balance of the cosmos."

"Why should that matter?" thundered the avatar of death. "Too many blasphemies have been committed against me. Immortals have come into my domain to steal my secrets and my own subjects were taken away. I say to you: Enough!"

"But, er..."

"This is a waste of time," Rakar said, placing a hand on Ra's shoulder. "He won't listen. We were fools to ever trust him; he used me as a beacon to access our dimension, nothing more. The only way to avoid a catastrophe is to close the door we've unwittingly opened..."

Whispers rose amongst the Immortals. Some had fallen to their knees, face down, and were praying. Sebek himself did not know what to do. To the inhabitants of Heliopolis, Etarr was the ultimate god, the embodiment of a fate that remained alien to them. Ra gazed at them for a moment, then turned back to Rakar.

"I... I don't know what to do," he confessed.

"I see no way to close the passage," replied the shaman.

"There must be something we can try," said the Black Lys. "We can't give up now."

But only silence answered her. This time, the situation was desperate.

Blackie Sullivan watched the fine mist that intertwined around their feet, becoming more and more tangible. He passed his fingers through it and felt a tingling sensation.

"I do have an idea," he said. "Etarr's dimension is, in its own way, the opposite of ours. It is the domain of death, while our reality belongs to the living. It is like matter meeting antimatter..."

"That's about right," Rakar agreed. "From a mystical standpoint, anyway."

"Well, I'm the master of dark matter, and Jeff gets his powers from the cosmic energy around him. We're two opposing forces, too. If we could channel our respective powers and clash..."

"...Then the resulting explosion might be enough to completely sever Earth from the Realm of Shadows and return Etarr to his plane of reality," finished the Dark Flyer. "Fred, that's brilliant!"

"Except for one thing," said Jeff. "The Soul of Levan no longer obeys me..."

"And I no longer seem able to control dark matter," added Blackie.

"To concentrate your powers, you'd need, I don't know, some kind of super-accumulator...." said the Black Lys.

The Mysterious Archer took Ra's Medallion out of his backpack.

"Perhaps we've got one," he said. "I figured we shouldn't let this go to waste, so I grabbed it. If I remember correctly, didn't someone say that this jewel could contain the power of a supernova?"

"Yes!" Ra enthused. "It could work! We just need to restore the power of the Sullivans to its rightful owners."

"You and I can do it," said Rakar. "The way I see it, the Soul of Levan was disturbed by Jeff's return. It doesn't know how to handle two heirs simultaneously. Let's help it with my magic and your telepathy."

The Immortal nodded.

"What should we do?" asked Jeff.

The shaman issued his instructions. Time was of the essence, since Etarr consolidating his hold onto the Earth dimension.]

Jeff and Blackie placed themselves beneath the entity, one hand each on the Medallion. Behind them, Ra and Rakar closed their eyes and concentrated. They combined their powers to communicate with the Soul of Levan. The two brothers felt the souls of their companions entering them, seeking the strange entity that was their family's most precious gift.

"There it is," said Rakar. "Buried deep in Fred's soul..."

"I see it," confirmed the Immortal. "I'm going to talk to it, convince it to bless both Sullivans."

Fred felt the power of the Soul of Levan awakening within him, like a rush flooding every cell in his body. He felt his power over dark matter return...

But this time the Soul didn't stop with his body. It passed through the Medallion and filled Jeff in turn. The Man of Brass recognized the familiar feeling and soaked up the Soul's healing energy.

"Cendrine, you and the others should take shelter," he said. "This could be dangerous."

"Jukka, Dominik, Sweet and I can't help you, but we will support you to the end," replied the Black Lys.

"What she said," added the Dark Flyer, while the Mysterious Archer simply nodded.

"And we, too, will stay with our king!" Sebek shouted, his soldiers behind him.

All that confidence strengthened Jeff's resolve. A golden glow surrounded him. Beside him, Fred started to radiate a black aura.

"Ready?" asked the Man of Brass.

"I was waiting for you," Blackie replied, smiling.

With the same gesture, the two brothers brandished the Medallion of Ra and poured all their power into it.

Light and darkness mixed without mixing, creating a sphere like a Yin-Yang symbol encompassing both their bodies. All around, them the mist dissipated, as if driven away by a cosmic wind.

Then the Sullivans gave out a loud shout. For the first time, they, who had once been deadly enemies, and whose powers were diametrically opposed, drew on their differences and united to save the world.

Cosmic energy and dark matter collided and it was like another big bang! An intense light burst upon everything, before retracting to condense on the Medallion of Ra. A mighty ray burst out of it, straight up into the sky. When it reached the limits of the atmosphere, it spread around the planet and fell down in iridescent lines like a miracle rain. This chased away the deathly mist, and life returned to reality.

Etarr's face showed his fury, but even this cosmic being was powerless to counter the primal force that had once given birth to the universe. He, too, dissipated, like a drawing in the sand that the tide washes away.

Not a trace remained of Etarr the Inevitable in the land of the living.

Jeff and Fred had collapsed to the ground, barely able to stand up after this colossal effort.

"This time, he's gone for good," said Blackie.

"Yes, I felt it too," confirmed the Man of Brass."But I fear the Soul of Levan has left us, you as well as me. However, it looks as if I still have my powers, I don't understand why..."

"All that I have left are the powers I gained on Mars..."

Rakar and Ra helped them up. The Hexagoneers crowded around them, expressing their congratulations and cheers. The Immortals joined in this celebration. Yet Jeff's face remained gloomy.

"What is it?" Ra asked. "Is Etarr still here?"

"No," replied the Man of Brass. "But, Ben, I had access to your thoughts and your memories…"

The Immortal blanched.

The Man of Brass turned to face Sebek and his men.

"I've seen the crimes I committed while I was under Set's control," he said. "As Amon, I almost killed you and I murdered a good man, General Anhur. I must answer for these crimes."

"You can't blame yourself for these!" cried the Black Lys. "You weren't yourself. Set is the only one responsible."

But the Frenchwoman knew Jeff Sullivan's nature. She knew that he would never forgive himself.

"Nevertheless, this man is correct, and it is to his credit that he is not evading his responsibilities," Sebek intervened. "It is for the people of Heliopolis to judge him, just as Set and his other allies will be judged."

"About that…" Dominik said hesitantly.

The Hexagoneers and Immortals turned their attention to the prisoners, only to find out that one was missing. Athor and Bastet were still hampered and helpless, but Set had escaped!

"No way!" cried Sweet. "My mental virus should have neutralized him for several more hours!"

"Don't blame yourself," Ra said. "You won't be the last person to have underestimated my brother. I have often done it myself. He's taken advantage of the confusion to escape our vigilance, but even though he is free, he is alone and without resources."

"We're too exhausted to go after him," said the Black Lys. "The best thing we can do is to return to Heliopolis..".

The sense of triumph that everyone had felt when Set had been defeated was now tinted with a bittersweet flavor. Victory was not total and the latest events were to weigh heavily on Hexagon and its reborn founder.

The Hexajet took off and headed for Mount Zefidu It was as if the night had swallowed it, and the emotions its passengers felt.

EPILOGUE

The next few days passed in melancholy.

The Immortals and Hexagon had defeated Set and repelled Etarr, but Heliopolis had been hit hard during the battle against the Xans. The city was partially in ruins, and many of its inhabitants had perished. In a population so small, whose lives stretched for millennia, every death was a tragedy, a tremendous loss to the community.

A sober ceremony brought together the people of Heliopolis to pay tribute to the deceased, in particular to General Anhur, a true hero in the eyes of his people. The Hexagoneers were allowed to attend as honorary citizens, but Jeff Sullivan wisely chose not to be there, feeling that his presence would have been inappropriate.

Athor and Bastet were tried and declared traitors to Heliopolis. They were sentenced to be locked up in an underground prison—a particularly cruel punishment for Immortals.

The Medallion of Ra had been broken when the energies of Jeff and Fred had poured into it, but its fragments were nevertheless taken back to the Arsenal. The *Book of the Dead* would join them as soon as the city's scientists had finished analyzing it.

Finally, a small council met to decide the case of Jeff Sullivan. Osir, Sebek, Isis and a few other notables sat on it; Ra, however, had declined to participate, arguing that he lacked objectivity. After a single session, the council decided unanimously that Jeff could not be held responsible for the crimes committed by Amon, all the more so in light of his role in the defeat of Set and Etarr.

All the Hexagoneers were relieved, but Jeff retained a measure of guilt, an indelible stain on his heroic soul.

Finally, it was time to leave Heliopolis. Ra took the decision to go with the rest of his team. He felt he had dragged his comrades into a personal conflict and wished to continue to work alongside them to thank them for their help.

Rakar was looking forward to seeing Kathryn again, and Jeff to seeing both his wife and daughter—especially after learning that he was soon going to be a grandfather!

On the eve of their departure, a grand party was held to honor the heroes who had defended Heliopolis as if it were their own.

Blackie Sullivan had secluded himself on a balcony, away from the hustle and bustle of the banquet. The fresh air of that early evening caressed his face—a pleasant sensation. He had decisions to make, and questions to answer.

He felt his brother's presence behind him. The Man of Brass leaned against the parapet beside him.

"Cendrine told me that you want to leave the team," said Jeff.

"That's right."

"You don't have to. You proved yourself when I wasn't there. You deserve your place."

"I joined Hexagon because I felt I owed it to you. It was a first step on my road to redemption. Now that you're back, I feel that I have to move on."

"What are you going to do?"

"I don't know yet," Fred replied with a shrug. "I'll probably travel around the world for a while. Maybe start my own team, who knows? I have a lot of wrongs to right."

"Listen Fred, when we shared memories, I saw what you did for Kathryn. You fought for her, you protected her when I wasn't there to do it. I'll never forget that."

The two men looked at each other for a moment. There was a heavy debt between them and all the accumulated grudge of years could not disappear so quickly. But tonight, for the first time in years, they could just be brothers and not rivals. They shook hands, their hearts filled with a comforting feeling.

Never before had the Soul of Levan to face such a challenge. It had stretched to the extreme between two heirs—an unprecedented situation.

When the explosion had occurred, the energy of the Sullivans had been scattered but now it was unified again. Yet the singularity remained. It had been split in two for a brief moment, and carried it like a stigma.

The Soul of Levan rose into the ether, seeking a Sullivan—two Sullivans? It didn't know anymore. But it knew that when it would find the rightful host—hosts—it would not hesitate for a moment.

The Sullivan legacy would live on!

Kathryn Sullivan was washing the dishes from the lunch she just had shared with her mother. She drew a certain sense of peace serenity from this mundane task. It had been several days since she last had heard from Francis, who had left with Hexagon after the Battle of New York. She didn't worry too much because Rakar was no pushover and the rest of Hexagon was with him.

But her inactivity weighed on her and she couldn't help wondering what the team was doing.

Suddenly, she feels a tension in her belly. She smiled, passes a soft hand over the blossoming roundness.

"Patience, you kids," she said aloud. "You will soon be free."

She suddenly felt overwhelmed by an incomparable sense of well-being. A gentle euphoria filled her soul and it was as if the universe itself had penetrated every pore of her skin.

But after that feeling of elation came pain. A violent contraction drew a moan out of her. She took a step back and leaned against the table. Her thighs suddenly felt wet—her water had broken!

Panic and joy mingled in her mind.

"Mom!" shouted Kathryn Sullivan. "The twins are coming!"

THE GUARDIAN OF THE THRESHOLD

GALLERY

Many of the characters featured in this book have previously appeared (and will continue to appear) in Hexagon Comics titles.

As mentioned in our introduction, the Hexagon Group itself starred in two eponymous comics featuring Jeff and Fred Sullivan (whose career started as a villain in the *Max Tornado* series), the Black Lys, the Dark Flyer, the Mysterious Archer and others. They also appeared in *Strangers* 1, which recounts the story of Jeff's death on the Moon.

The Dark Flyer and Sweet, as well as Kathryn Sullivan (Plasma), also appeared in *Strangers* 2 and 3.

Ben Leonard (Ra), as well as the Black Lys, the Dark Flyer and Mozam, returned in *The Enchanters*, a story which actually takes place after this novel. And the evil Set has since also returned in a couple of recent issues of *Strangers*, yet to be translated.

NYPD Detective Trumbo (from the team of Galton & Trumbo) last appeared in the Sibilla one-shot included in our recent *Phenix / Sibilla* comic.

The Lakota mage Ozark guest-starred in *Strangers* 3; Moemi the witch appeared in one of the stories collected in *Zembla* 1; the Guardian of the Threshold recently made an appearance in *Strangers*.

Other characters mentioned in this book have yet to appear in any English-language translations. The parallel world of Erden, divided between Flyers and Crawlers, was introduced in *The Other*, a sequel to *Wampus* yet to be translated, and recently played an important part in the Season 5 of *Strangers*.

The endearing team of Jill & John were only ever featured in one story published in 1983 and this is the first time they returned.

In the following pages, we provide a gallery of images featuring these characters taken from the comics.

Jean-Marc Lofficier

BLACK
LYS

DARK FLYER

SWEET

MYSTERIOUS ARCHER

RAKAR

BLACKIE SULLIVAN

RÂ

JEFF SULLIVAN

MOEMI

OZARK